NEW MAPS

deindustrial fiction

VOL. 2, NO. 4
FALL 2022

LOOSELEAF PUBLISHING

Bayfield, Wisconsin

About *New Maps*

New Maps publishes stories in the growing genre of deindustrial fiction, which explores the long decline of industrial civilization, its aftermath, and the new worlds made possible by its departure. The magazine also publishes essays, book reviews, letters to the editor, and other content that examines these themes. For more on the philosophy of the magazine, see the website below, or get acquainted by way of this issue.

Submissions of any of the foregoing may be addressed to the editor at either of the addresses below. Story submission guidelines may be found on the website or requested by post.

New Maps is published quarterly by Looseleaf Publishing. Subscriptions are currently available in the U.S., Australia, Belgium, Canada, Germany, Hong Kong, Ireland, Japan, the Netherlands, New Zealand, Sweden, and the U.K. An annual subscription is $48.00 USD for U.S. addresses, with different prices elsewhere, and may be purchased from the website below, or by writing to request an order form.

Postal correspondence:
Looseleaf Publishing
87095 Valley Road
Bayfield, WI 54814, USA

Online:
www.new-maps.com
editor@new-maps.com

ISSN: 2767-388X

Image credits:

— Cover art © 2022 by Bruna Nobrega.
— Photo on p. 26 © 2022 by Nathanael Bonnell.
— Photos on p. 27 © 2022 by Ann Troxel.
— Image on p. 31 © 2022 by Pierre Magdelaine.

Contents

Introduction

Ah, fall, the time of the year when, up here, everyone tries to get done everything they didn't finish during the summer before they lose the opportunity under three feet of snow. If fall isn't deftly managed, things quickly get hard to manage … which is why this issue is a bit later than usual.

Timing notwithstanding, this issue features six terrific stories that I'm excited to share. The synchronicities that happen while I put this magazine together are always interesting, too. Justin Patrick Moore, Wesley Stine (in the Letters), and I have all, in this magazine's nonfiction pieces, approached from different angles the topic of the importance of thinking in many different ways. Which is especially tidy because it illustrates the larger point.

Looseleaf Publishing has been busy since summer, finishing the release of a new standalone book, the amply titled *The Flesh of Your Future Sticks Between My Teeth: Stories from the* Gristle *Cli-fi Parody Contest*. Edited by John Michael Greer, it's a collection of twelve razor-sharp parodies of the conventional wisdom of our time that holds that "raising awareness" and being "intersectional" will solve all the world's problems. Check it out at Looseleaf's new website, www.looseleaf.pub.

This issue concludes the second year of *New Maps*! So **remember to renew** your subscription if it's expiring at the end of this year. (If you don't know when yours expires, you can always write to orders@new-maps.com to ask.) Now when you renew you can get an auto-renewing subscription, and won't have to remember to come back each year. (One-time subscriptions are still available.)

And on a less commercial note, *thank you* to everyone who's supported this magazine through subscriptions and individual orders. It's been a great two years, and I'm looking forward to the next.

—*Nathanael Bonnell*
Editor

Letters

New Maps welcomes letters, whether to the editor or as part of a conversation between readers in the Letters section. Email editor@new-maps.com, *with "Letter" somewhere in the subject line, and sign with your name as you'd like it to be printed. Or write via post, including your name and a note to consider your letter for publication, to Looseleaf Publishing, 87095 Valley Road, Bayfield, WI 54814, USA.*

I really enjoyed the Summer issue of *New Maps*. Every story was a winner. Entertaining, imaginative, packing a punch or slinging a zinger in the reader's direction. It was like crossing a big river on a series of well-spaced, happily placed stepping stones. With all the changes going on around me and within me, these crisply written envisionings of what might come to be gave me a sensation of having a more secure footing in a wide rushing wilderness of water. High, dry, flat, & broad enough to stand on and catch my breath. Able to hold still for a moment before taking the next step and the next. None of the stories required a leap too far for my old feet and dodgy knees. Not one of the rocks was wobbly underfoot. Thanks, y'all!

I like the intermixing of the factual material and photos too. I played around with some calculations about electric cars, based on D. England's piece. If there should be just one 'Lectro-Car for every 5 households, or roughly one per suburban block, then the lithium required for one year's worth of cars would come to about one-third of the U.S. holdings. But just how likely is it that people in the U.S are going to carpool or ride-share, rent, or co-own a neighborhood 'Lectro-Car?

Ehhnnnnnzzzt! (negatory buzzer sound). Not gonna happen.

Say, if a 'Lectro-Car has a range of 200 miles does that mean it would take a string of 13 or 14 of them to complete a relay race from Ocracoke, NC to Oakland, CA? How do they handle in wet weather? In high heat? We could skip most of Texas by cutting across just the Panhandle, but what about Death Valley? Would regenerative braking give the vehicles just a little extra juice for more distance? Dunno. Maybe there is a story in there somewhere.

Across the States in 10 Lightning Bugs! The cars have a fiberglass chassis shaped and painted like a fleet of 7-spot coccinella ladybugs, or green-glowing phosphor-tailed fireflies. They compete against a whole set of other transports within their 200-mile radius: electric assist bikes, sail-scooters, Pony Express, Olympic runners, little old ladies delivering biscuits in pedaled cargo bikes, hot air balloons ... I say, where is Jules Verne when you need him? Wish I was better at math calcs.

G. Kay Bishop

Dear G. Kay,
You might be interested to know that the British motorhead TV show Top Gear

did an episode in 2007 where four of the show's presenters raced from one end of London to the other in different vehicles: a nice car, a preposterously overpowered motorboat, a racing bicycle, and the Tube. The bicyclist won. The host, Jeremy Clarkson, who'd been throttling the boat down the Thames at 70 mph, found him already at their meeting place and in the ensuing discussion told him, "You've ruined Top Gear." In a few minutes they were joined by the Tube rider, and the car driver showed up a full 15 minutes after the others. That was a gas car (or, I suppose, a petrol car); I guess London might not challenge the range of one of today's electric cars, but imagine the ignominy if that 15-minute deficit were compounded by having to plug in the car awhile, or change mounts. Anyway I'll take the little old lady with the biscuits any day, especially if that's biscuits as the British define them.

(As for Lightning Bugs, well, Volkswagen is starting production this year on an electric version of its iconic microbus, calling it the Buzz ...)

Glad you liked the issue! I'm glad this magazine can serve as a stepping-and-standing stone. Goodness knows we need that sort of thing in this kind of historical moment. —NB

☉

Editor,

One of the pleasures of reading (and writing) deindustrial fiction comes from the sheer variety of perspectives to which it can give voice. And this wonderful variety is what we get when we treat the fossil-fueled present as what it is — just one historical era out of many, which will in all likelihood be followed by a deindustrial future just as long and fascinating as the preindustrial past.

I think that even many writers of conventional sci-fi have realized, at some level, that simply projecting the technoscape of the 20th century into the distant future puts their stories into a sort of straitjacket. And this is why we so often see the authors of stories set in outer space coming up with ways to knock their cultures down the scale a bit, into more fertile ground.

Most of my readers are probably aware of Frank Herbert's Dune series, in which the Butlerian Jihad and the ensuing taboo on making "a machine in the likeness of the human mind" lead to a lot of cultural diversity, as the characters seek new ways to plumb the depths of their human potential.

Another, more obscure specimen of the "mixed-tech space tale" occurs in one of my own favorite novels, Orson Scott Card's *Worthing Chronicle*, when the frozen passengers of a colony ship have their memories wiped out in a space battle while en route to their destination planet. Since only the pilot retains knowledge of the colonists' high-tech homeworld, he must content himself with building a neo-medieval society, in which a few wonders from the starship survive amid a lot of rediscovered agrarian lore.

(Curiously enough, as I was writing the last paragraph I realized that another one of my favorites, Vernor Vinge's *A Fire upon the Deep*, employs almost the same gimmick — all of a spaceship's adults, save one, are killed in battle after landing on a new planet; that one, plus the children, must build a new society alongside the planet's natives — a medieval, wolflike race on the cusp of experiencing their own scientific revolution.)

Of course, when writing deindustrial fiction, it isn't necessary to rely upon Butlerian Jihads or mass memory loss to obtain an excuse for building societies with a creative mix of new and old technology. We can just cite the depletion of fossil fuels, which is already happening all around us, and the simmering decline and eventual fall of the civilization in which we live.

And the events of the last three years have made it a lot harder for observant people to hide from that decline.

As for myself, I barely squeaked into the deindustrial scene before the events of 2020 propelled us all into the flashy present phase of the world's reordering. It was in early 2019 that I adopted a loosely deindustrial worldview, with its "winter is coming" mentality, its lack of faith in political solutions, its conviction that decades of mostly papered-over economic and social deterioration will eventually give way to something harder to hide from, and its belief that new cultures can one day be built on the rubble, but only after enough people have renounced both their passivity and their feelings of entitlement.

Also, surprising as it may seem, I had arrived at this basic worldview before I came to believe that peak oil, resource depletion in general, and climate change were serious problems.

I had already learned enough, in my studies of the United States' political economy, to realize that something was deeply wrong — that real economic output (when you look past the cloud of misleading GDP and inflation statistics) had been declining at least since the 1990s, that once-thriving manufacturing centers had disappeared in favor of paper-pushing and sketchily financed imports, and that young men's nonparticipation in work, marriage, and homeownership was at all time highs.

And because I was still swimming in the half-Reaganite, half-libertarian, Ron Paulish belief system in which I had been raised, I blamed all of this on overregulation, on monetary policy that encourages imports in lieu of domestic production, on an education system that adapts people for lives as office plankton rather than as makers of tangible goods, and on broken or absent families that fail to raise disciplined and hardworking young men.

Later on, I broke with the Republican Party on the climate change/peak oil issue. And here I am.

My new "discoveries" regarding climate and resource limits did not, at a deep level, change my belief that our society is headed for some sort of collapse. They just added more detail to the picture. The conclusions I had reached before were still valid — if you want to understand why life has been so rough for so many Americans these days, then bureaucratic bloat, fiat money, and the intensely untraditional environment in which children are raised are still big pieces of the puzzle.

And if you take a look around, you'll find plenty of people out there in much the same situation in which I once was — people who are dismissive and/or indifferent to the issues most commonly discussed by the readership of *New Maps*, but who still have a pretty good grasp on one or more elements of the ongoing decline. For instance, there were plenty of people out there who never cared much about carbon emissions, yet who had a strong opinion that it was a bad idea for scientists to try to anticipate the next pandemic by collecting bat viruses and deliberately modifying them to infect human beings, and who expected that the human race would eventually face consequences for mucking about with forces of nature that are best left alone.

The whole situation is somewhat like the old fable of the blind men and the elephant. Each man feels a different part of the elephant, and comes to a different conclusion about the elephant's shape. "It is like a spear," says the man who feels the tusk. "No, the elephant clearly resembles rope," says the man feeling the tail. And so forth. They argue loudly about it, and they can't come to any shared consensus. But at the end of the day, there really is an elephant, and the men's descriptions are all partly in the right.

So it is with the demise of the present social order. If you search out prominent voices talking about collapse and eventual rebirth, you will find a menagerie of different opinions focused on very different aspects of the events in question. These voices will include both innovators and traditionalists, people all over the political not-a-spectrum and people who prefer to ignore politics, followers of a variety of religions and followers of no religion at all.

You will hear a lot of different things, some of which will surprise you. (For instance, I recall having a long conversation once with a man who thought everything had started going downhill with the disappearance of good investigative journalists in the 1980s). And ultimately, you will find yourself agreeing with at least some of these surprising things, and incorporating them into your own mental map of the world.

Though I may be wrong, it seems to me that most people in the *New Maps* community are lifelong environmentalists who arrived at the deindustrial worldview after becoming disillusioned with the political Left. My perspective is somewhat different, since I got here after becoming disillusioned with the Right.

But even though I now feel quite negatively about my erstwhile comrades' willingness to believe comforting myths about the sustainability of the fossil-fueled economy (as well as comforting myths about a lot of other things), I have still held on to much of my old worldview. And I think that by the time the rubble stops bouncing, and we've all been compelled, in one way or another, to feel a lot more of the elephant, all of these rival factions (my own included) will have come closer to-gether.

In the coming age of scarcity, people with traditional views about work, family, and chastity will likely admit that burning through fossil fuels the way we all once did was a moral problem much like all the others they had been inveighing against. At the same time, a loss of control over pregnancies and venereal diseases will lead a lot of people on the other side of things to come around to the idea that the sexual revolution was a mistake, and that there are reasons why societies that are built to last usually demand that young people bridle their passions. And so forth.

In the meantime, may we all continue to enjoy the eclectic offerings of *New Maps*, and of whatever other out-of-the-mainstream publications each of us has had the good fortune to discover. And may we do so in the knowledge that the most certain thing about the elephant is that nobody has felt the whole elephant!

Wesley,

The diversity of perspectives is one of my favorite things about deindustrial fiction as well. I've always had a bad allergy to the monoculturizing tendency of the fossil fuel age. It's weird, really, that at least in the U.S., kids in English class are given a diet of books like Brave New World, 1984, The Giver, *and (in my school, though perhaps unusually)* Ayn Rand's Anthem, *which all extol the virtue of thinking differently from the lumpen sheeple—while our culture at large gives us the exact opposite message: that America is a melting pot, and all types of people are welcome so long as they sign on to go to sleep and dream the American Dream. (The irony is even sharper in the public school system, which takes homogenization as not just a virtue but practically a* raison d'être.) The Great Gatsby *still gets taught in schools too, a* book that tries to show that money and social status don't confer happiness, but one century-old book apparently loses the fight about 99 times out of 100 against the weight of the young reader's entire culture.

Actually that book didn't particularly help jog me out of the conventional paradigm; I read it and mostly forgot it once I took the test. If any book helped, it might, oddly enough, have been Daniel Pinkwater's The Snarkout Boys and the Avocado of Death, a YA novel that I still reread now and then. Two high-school misfits meet, start sneaking out of their houses at night to an all-night movie theater, begin meeting eccentrics, then find themselves investigating a bizarre mystery in which old German cinema is used as a torture tool and a supercomputer made from a sentient avocado threatens to bring the world to an awful fate. I didn't need to be shown the consequences of the conventional way, but the rewards of stepping outside it into something weird, something completely free of that constraint.

Really I don't know if I should credit books, or upbringing, or past lives, or what, for the fact that I've felt sufficiently self-possessed to do things like hitchhike around for years or move to an off-grid cabin. But in any case it's clear to me that there's an amazing riotous diversity to the ways you can go once you swim out of the mainstream. When I was younger, I was interested in all that just because it was so fun. Now that I'm older, I realize that all

those divergent paths are also, in fact, useful to humanity—in ways more profound than almost anything the mainstream can claim. They are the embodiment of dissensus, the idea that to get through an uncertain time, the best response is a vast number of different responses, on the theory that at least one of them will turn out to be successful. Dissensus is the diversity of forms from which evolution brings new species, new ideas, into existence.[1]

So when people bring the perspectives of their different backgrounds to the task of imagining the deindustrial future, I'm all for it. I suspect you're right that current readers of this magazine have started out mostly as people interested in the environment; I'd have to count myself among that number. But those who started out as you did—seeing the evidence of societal degradation, and trying to work out where it's coming from and where it's going—and those who have arrived from some other starting point entirely, all help deindustrial fiction feature less of the kind of monocropped hack-fiction futures that proliferate in the mainstream, and make it into more of an accurate guess at where we're going. We won't get there on the main roads.

Readers—what early political, philosophical, or cultural leanings of yours eventually made you find your way here? And what other "out-of-the-mainstream publications" do you look to for valuable insight on the gathering collapse and the future after it? —NB

---

1 See John Michael Greer's "Dissensus and Organic Processes," The Archdruid Report, June 2017. archdruidmirror.blogspot.com/2017/06/dissensus-and-organic-process.html

ESSAYS & SUNDRIES

The Power of Three

Ternary Logic, Triolectics, and Football

If we continue to operate in terms of a Cartesian dualism of mind versus matter, we shall probably also continue to see the world in terms of God versus man; elite versus people; chosen race versus others; nation versus nation; and man versus environment. It is doubtful whether a species having both an advanced technology and this strange way of looking at its world can endure.
— Gregory Bateson, "The Cybernetics of 'Self':
A Theory of Alcoholism" (1971)

Beyond the Cartesian Duel

Binary thinking seems to be a plague visited upon mankind, locking our minds into grooves that oscillate between the extremes of yes or no, true or false, love or hate, good or evil, left or right, black or white, communism or capitalism, utopia or oblivion, leaving little room to explore variances on the spectrum between polar opposites. This habit creates false dilemmas when all the available options get reduced down

Cheap Thrills
*Speculations on
Entertainment, Media,
Art, and Leisure in the
Deindustrial Age*
Justin Patrick Moore

to just two. Entire fields of possibility are left unexplored. When our minds identify with just one pole it tends to create fundamentalist antagonisms towards people and institutions whose thinking centers on the opposite pole. When we ignore the vast terrain of middle ground that lies between, like ignoring the experience of those who live in the flyover states between the coasts, we miss out on many nuanced realms of meaning. The worst aspect of binary thinking is probably the deleterious effect it has on our ability to imagine what may yet be possible.

Polarities do exist, and they often exert tremendous tugs at one another, as in the polarities of magnets, of male and female. When the polarities in question are political or religious in nature it animates the animus and people tend to slip into acrimony. The increased animosity between liberal Democrats and conservative Republicans over the past decade or more is a case in point. On some deep level I think they subconsciously get off on this attraction to each other. The foaming mouth of a fundamentalist Christian denouncing heavy metal, role playing games, and gay sex is as often as not projecting their shadow side onto

9

the object of their hate. By the same token an angry anti-gun activist may harbor secret wishes to wield destructive powers over others. Is there a way out of these twin blind alleys of diametrical opposition? Can we find healing from our collective bipolar disorder?

I think there is a way and it can be found at the fulcrum, the center point of the scales, the point of perfect balance and integration between two opposing poles. We can take steps towards moving to that fulcrum by exploring philosophy, in the form of ternary logic and triolectics, and by playing games designed for three teams, in this case Three-Sided Football.

In the past philosophy wasn't just a way for academics to get tenure. Serious contributions to philosophy and science came from engaged citizens who weren't tied to publishing and pushing papers on regular basis just to keep their position. As "dollar dollar bills y'all" became the name of the academic game, theories seem to have become increasingly harebrained, existing only within the phantasmal realm of a mirrored echo chamber. Universities continue to flounder, and the study of philosophy, including the philosophy of science, is a suitable pastime for those downwardly mobile dandies who don't want to get their hands dirty on mudlarking expeditions, but would rather get lost in thought as they drift about as aspiring flâneurs. They will have to be willing to dirty up their minds, however, as mind is not separate from nature, as the Cartesian dualists would have people to think.

An Ecological Injection of Ternary Logic

Charles Sanders Peirce (1839–1914) was an American philosopher, mathematician, logician and scientific thinker. His father, Benjamin Peirce, was also of scientific bent, and was a professor of astronomy and mathematics at Harvard University. Growing up in an environment of high intellectual achievement honed Peirce's considerable natural gifts, and a career in academia was almost a given for him, if he hadn't scandalized the prim and proper minds at Johns Hopkins University. His teaching job there was terminated without warning due to the fact that he was living in sin with his second wife, Juliette Annette Froissy, a.k.a. Juliette Annette Pourtalai, before the divorce from his first was official. Juliette also happened to be Romani, and her heritage was another mark of prejudice against the couple. This fall from the graces of higher learning left him unemployable at other universities. He ended up eking out a living by writing for scientific journals, crafting entries for *Century Dictionary*, and doing intermittent work for the U.S. Coast and Geodetic Survey. When his father passed away he was left with enough inheritance to buy a farmhouse on property near Milford, Pennsylvania, where the couple was able to remain independently poor. Their poverty was not quite genteel, but it did allow him to be extremely prolific in his writing, much of which is still unpublished. He often had to write on the reverse of manuscript pages because he was at times unable to afford fresh paper.

As the university system implodes, those who have an interest in philosophy, science, or other academic pursuits could do worse than follow Peirce's example, and continue to study, write and publish as independent scholars.

Thinking in terms of threes seemed to be natural to Peirce. Triads, trichotomies, and groupings of threes are found throughout his work. His system of logic consisted of three parts: speculative grammar, speculative rhetoric, and what he called critic. He also sketched out a formal system of math based on triadic logic. Peirce is also credited as the philosopher who kick-started the contemporary study of semiotics, or the general study of signs and signification, representation and meaning.[1] Peirce defined a sign as being triadic, composed of three parts, these being the sign vehicle, the object and the interpretant.

Peirce had suffered from the painful effects of facial neuralgia, a condition he had since his teenage years, which may have been partially responsible for the couple's relative social isolation. Yet out of his suffering came the gift of his prodigious thinking and his obsession with logic. Peirce believed that some propositions in logic are neither true nor false. He rejected the Principle of Bivalence that states that any proposition can only be false or true. This provided the motivation he needed to pursue triadic solutions.

In his concentrated thought Peirce was led to create a triadic logic of induction, deduction and abduction. Induction is an inference that is probable, while deduction is a type of inference where the conclusion is supposed to follow necessarily from the premise. In a deduction it is impossible for the premise to be true and a conclusion to be false. Abduction is the process of inference by which a hypothesis can be generated and formed. This term is also sometimes called retroduction, and can be further defined as a way for researchers to conceptualize that requires them to identify those circumstances the concept cannot exist without. Peirce took these even further than logical argument forms and used them as the basis for truth-seeking that he called "scientific method." In his thought, induction, deduction and abduction become the three phases of scientific inquiry.[2]

---

1   Ferdinand de Saussure, who founded the modern study of linguistics, is considered the co-founder of semiotics alongside Peirce.

2   Gregory Bateson (1904–1980) was another gifted thinker who admired the work of Peirce. He adopted Peirce's triad of deduction, induction, and abduction as the best type of logic to use in conjunction with the scientific method.

Triolectic Mind Games

Just as philosophy contributes to the practice of science, so too can it contribute to the practice of art. Enter Danish painter and philosopher Asger Jorn (1914–1973), a co-founder of the Situationist International. In the early 1950s, after convalescing in a sanitorium where he was being treated for tuberculosis, Jorn wrote the text *Held og hasard* ("Luck and Chance"). He submitted this to the University of Copenhagen, which he hoped would approve it as a thesis. The text, however, was too unconventional. In it he argued that alongside the two dominant modes of thinking, philosophy and science, there was a third, valid alternative: an artistic mode. As per the title, he also wrote extensively on the role of luck and chance in all manner of situations.

In Jorn's text he speculated on how humans first learned to walk, and cited Erik Nyholm, who believed the first humans were apes who had learned to sing, due to a new jaw structure that allowed for more movement of the tongue, which in turn allowed for the creation of new sounds. Singing became an incitement to dance, and dancing distinguished early humans from other animals. Singing and dancing apes learned to walk by first learning to dance on their hind legs. From this perspective, Jorn suggested that game playing is a way to enter new stages of evolutionary change. The inclination towards pleasure and fun is an incitement to new behaviors. Games are also very often subject to the role, or roll, of chance, which brings about novel experiences.

Peirce had also been an advocate of chance and its role in evolution. He thought that chance, what he termed Tyche[3], or Tychism, "must give birth to an evolutionary cosmology, in which all the regularities of nature and of mind are regarded as products of growth."

The Situationists espoused many interventions to break people away from the trance of the society of the spectacle. Games were used to break apart the rigid binary of work time and leisure time. They strove to show how play was not just a way to spend "free time" in the off hours away from office, factory, or cashiers register, but a way to transform existing energies and put them to use on life giving activities.

Asger Jorn had long been smitten with Hegelian and Marxist dialectics. While the dialectic method of philosophical argument can be traced back to Plato, and was used under the rubric of medieval logic, it was given a new lease on intellectual life when G. W. F. Hegel made it a core aspect of reality itself. Karl Marx and Friedrich Engels then got a hold of it and further retooled it into dialectical materialism. As communism spread, the idea of dialectical materialism

---

3   "Tyche, in Greek religion, the goddess of chance, with whom the Roman Fortuna was later identified; a capricious dispenser of good and ill fortune."

became a major part of the intellectual ecology of the era, and Jorn was among those who became enamored.

Jorn, however, saw many restrictions in dialectical materialism. As a writer, philosopher, and theorist he tinkered on it, blending in his own ideas, and attempted to extend it with insights from quantum physics. What he came up with was Triolectics, a playful rebuke. In time, due to a thought experiment in his book *Natural Order*, it became the basis for Three-Sided Football[4].

Three-sided Football

Jorn came up with the game of Three-Sided Football (TSF) as an outgrowth of his writings on Triolectical Materialism. These were first written about in his pamphlet, "De la méthode triolectique dans ses applications en situlogie générale" ("The Application of the Triolectical Method in General Situology") published by the Scandinavian Institute of Comparative Vandalism.[5] According to the members of the team Strategic Optimism Football, triolectics "went beyond linear transfers of energy, constructing spatio-temporal fields of possibility and negotiation. Not oppositional but superpositional — contradictions resolved by blending multiple simultaneous potentialities."

For Jorn, Three-Sided Football was just a thought-experiment, a way to play with the philosophy behind Triolectics. In *Natural Order*, he wrote,

> Let three teams meet on a six-angled plane instead of a rectangular one ... First of all one wants to quickly discover that it is impossible to control who of the two enemies attacking is shooting the goal. It becomes necessary to turn the rules around ... so that the victorious side is the side that has best defended themselves, and where the fewest goals have been let in. The victory has become defensive and not offensive ... It will not at all be an exciting match ... a third force can in this way neutralize a tension between two forces. That is why two-sided opponents are always aggressive or attack-minded, while three-sided are defensive. Whether this in itself marks a transition from dialectic to complementarity, I would like to leave unsaid. ... There are in these observations absolutely no political suggestions. I am only searching to find out what is actually going on ... Whether

---

4   And by football I mean soccer.
5   In May and June of 1963 Jorn traveled around Norway with the French photographer Gérard Franceschi. They documented the millennia-old tradition of Nordic folk art in a massive archive of over 25,000 photos. These now form the main collection of the Skandinavisk Institut for Sammenlignende Vandalisme ("Scandinavian Institute for Comparative Vandalism"), which the pair founded together in 1961.

a triangular relationship is static or constant, that would depend on whether there is an increasing tension. In that case this might lead to a real explosion, whereas the possibilities in the two-sided relationship are cancelled out by the two-sided fight's neverending energy use.

Such insights from Triolectics could be useful to those who want to escape the state of advanced rigor mortis that seems to be the inevitable byproduct of the forever culture war.

In the 1990s a number of post-Situationist groups began to bubble up in the UK and Europe. Psychogeography and détournement[6] were the prime interests. In the writings of the Situationists they had found a still valid critique of art and the leftist politics artists so often kept as bedfellows. At an anarchist event in Glasgow in 1994 Jorn's football thought-experiment descended from the Platonic realm of ideas, and the first actual games were played. Since then it has been played at different locations around the world. A World Cup for three-sided football was even organized at Jorn's hometown of Silkeborg, Denmark.

The game is pretty much played the way Jorn sketched it out. The winner of a TSF match is the team who gives up the fewest goals. If your team scores zero goals, it can still win, as long as the other teams gave up more goals than yours. The three teams play on a hexagonal pitch with three goal areas. Instead of splitting the time of the game into halves, it is played for a duration of three twenty-minute thirds. As the teams strive to concede as few goals as possible, various alliances are formed and dissolved in swift and fluid formations. With its roots in philosophical anarchism, the rest of the rules are flexible in the extreme, and a number of variations are played within the small TSF community.

The members of the Strategic Optimism Football team contend that the playing of the game teaches a way of strategy that removes two-sided oppositions. "Strategy is no longer the illusion of mastering a totality. Rather it is the negotiation of undecidables that removes both the binary fixity of formal Aristotelian logic and the teleology of dialectical change at once. One is presented not with the binary and fixed categories construed by media-imposed ideology. Rather one can glimpse an externality—the larger matrix of general emergencies that contain and triangulate the particular emergency."

As the world struggles to find solutions for our many crises and predicaments, ternary logic and triolectics can help individuals and communities escape from the rat race of us-against-them, and develop defensive survival strategies. For those of us who seek liberation from political binaries, and the Cartesian binary thinking that has divided humanity's experience and made it somehow

---

6   See my column "Walking in the Drift" in *New Maps* No. 2:1 (Winter 2022).

apart from nature, we could do much worse than to spend time playing games of ternary logic inside our heads, and games made for three teams with our friends. If we engage with our fellows in an interplay of imagination, we might just catch glimpses of the futures that lie beyond oblivion or utopia.

Re/sources

Illuminating more than just these brief snippets of the deep thoughts of Charles Sanders Peirce and Asger Jorn is beyond the scope of this essay. They are all worth digging into for those who want to explore further. Reading and contemplation are among the cheapest of pastimes, especially if you access material through your local library system. In my original sketch of this essay I had included information on the three-sided chess variant. It didn't end up fitting in the space allocated here. Readers may find it easier to organize a three-sided chess match than a three-sided football match, but the philosophical underpinnings differ.

The Art Story. "Asger Jorn: Danish Painter and Scholar." Accessed September 2022.
     https://www.theartstory.org/artist/jorn-asger/
Bateson, Gregory. *Steps to an Ecology of Mind.* New York, N.Y.: Ballantine, 1972.
     ↪ Bateson's essay *"The Cybernetics of 'Self': A Theory of Alcoholism"* is contained within this quintessential collection of his work that traverses across the disciplines of anthropology, psychiatry, evolution and genetics, systems theory, and ecology.
Burch, Robert. "Charles Sanders Peirce." *The Stanford Encyclopedia of Philosophy,* Edward N. Zalta (ed.). Stanford, Calif.: Metaphysics Research Lab, 2022.
     https://plato.stanford.edu/archives/sum2022/entries/peirce/
Colapietro, Vincent M. *Glossary of Semiotics.* New York, N.Y.: Paragon House, 1993.
     ↪ A useful text for anyone interested in semiotics. It contains many definitions of the abstruse terminology employed by Peirce.
Information Philosopher (website). "Charles Sanders Peirce" and "Gregory Bateson."
     https://informationphilosopher.com/solutions/philosophers/peirce/,
     https://informationphilosopher.com/solutions/scientists/bateson/.
     ↪ The Information Philosopher website, hosted and written by Bob Doyle, is a massive resource on philosophy and science as seen through the lens of information analysis.
Jorn, Asger. *The Natural Order and other Texts,* trans. Peter Shield. New York, N.Y.: Taylor and Francis, 2017.
Peirce, Charles Sanders. *The Essential Peirce,* eds. Nathan Houser and Christian Kloesel. Bloomington, Ind.: Indiana University Press, 1992.
Rasmussen, Mikkel Bolt, and Jakob Jakobsen, eds. *Cosmonauts of the Future: Texts from the Situationist Movement in Scandinavia and Elsewhere.* Brooklyn, N.Y.: Autonomedia, 2015.
Strategic Optimism Football (website). "Triolectical Materialism and the Beautiful Game of Three-Sided Football." https://strategicoptimismfootball →

.wordpress.com/2015/01/07/triolectical-materialism-and-the-beautiful-game-of-three-sided-football/

Parks, Tim. "Impossible Choices," ed. Nigel Warburton. Melbourne, Australia: Aeon, Jul. 15 2019. https://aeon.co/essays/gregory-bateson-changed-the-way-we-think-about-changing-ourselves
   ↪ A biographical essay on Bateson and his work.

Whither English?

(WITHER? ENGLISH?)

Riddle me this, oh my droogies. What is it that, yay, there it is snaky-sneakin' 'round in the back o' most o' these augurin's we spin here—and yet we unsee it and don't ref it, or at the most we unbigthink it?[1]

Editor's Soapbox

Nathanael Bonnell

Why yes: I'm thinking about the language itself in which the characters of deindustrial fiction stories speak, read, and think. The English we share these days isn't exactly the same as it was even in the 1980s, to say nothing of ye 1580s, and it will certainly have a somewhat different savor in the 2080s. We can't know exactly what turns it will take, but can we, perhaps, get a picture of the sorts of things likely to happen? All conclusions will be speculative, but this is a magazine devoted to speculation, so let's put some foundations under our forecasts and see where they lead.

The first thing to note is that English is going to change whether the collapse of industrial civilization proceeds at a slow and stately pace or gets everything done at once like a gallows drop; in fact it would assuredly change even if today's status quo were somehow maintained for centuries more or if those aliens who tear around our skies in blurry white ships finally condescended to give us the secret of interstellar travel. All languages change, all the time. It's inevitable enough a fact of life that there are linguists who reckon they've worked out the typical rate of change and can use it to date prehistoric events, like you might with other steady-rate processes like radioactive decay or mitochondrial DNA mutations.[2]

That said, though, the pace and the nature of the changes can vary quite a bit depending on, well, a lot of different things. Too, the things that change when languages change are often less obvious and more peculiar than you might guess if you've never peeked into the odd, dusty world inhabited by historical linguists.

Here's one counterintuitive thing to note right from the start. In the 1600s the main vehicles of mass information transmission were the newspaper and the book. In the 1700s, the main vehicles were the newspaper and the book, and in

---

1   Okay, I'll give away the answers: *A Clockwork Orange*, *Cloud Atlas*, and *1984*.

2   Having said that, I should acknowledge that glottochronology is not without controversy, and its detractors greatly doubt the precision it can give.

the 1800s they were the newspaper and the book (with the telephone gaining enough of a toehold before the turn of the century to rate a mention). The 1900s, though, brought a head-spinning succession of new ways to exchange information — affordable telephone sets, the radio, the phonograph, the fax, the television, the text message — until in the lead-up and the follow-up to the turn of the millennium the process reached a fever pitch with all the possibilities of the internet: websites, emails, chat groups, the erstwhile BBSes and listservs, memes, The Facebook, webinars, livestreaming, and whatever it is that TikTokkers do. You might think, then, that this orgy of telecommunication proliferation would carry a concomitant sea change in the way we speak. But for the most part, if you open a book from 1975, aside from an absence of URLs and a slightly greater occurrence of the word *groovy*, there won't actually be much to mark the language as different.

In fact what has happened has been exactly the reverse: with faster and more ubiquitous communication, not only has English largely failed to innovate, it has actually homogenized a great deal. In the early history of the U.S., for instance, different accents began to arise in different places, in the way they naturally do. Sometimes the accent's peculiar qualities were fueled by a large population of immigrants from some particular place, and sometimes they just sort of arose by chance. (The famous musicologist and freakazoid Harry Smith would some-times, at parties, ask people to sing a verse of the folk song "Barbara Allen," from which he could reliably pinpoint what county the singer was born in.)[3] When mass communication arrived on the scene, though, these accents quickly began to die out, replaced by what's been called "broadcast English" — the dialect that radio and TV announcers seem to speak no matter whether they're in Atlanta, Augusta, Anchorage, or Ann Arbor. A friend of mine maintains that "the elec-trification of rural America," and the broadcasts that followed, "was an act of genocide."

While it's true that the internet has spawned communities with all sorts of unique and obfuscatory ways of talking amongst themselves, it's also true that those ways of communicating are mostly limited to that particular corner of the internet. Rarely do they even get spoken aloud, much less make the leap into the common language. 4chan may be the source of an unsettlingly vast amount of internet content, but its mild argot has had a nearly negligible effect on English at large.

As it happens, easy transportation may have had even more to do with the flattening of English than broadcast did. Bill Bryson notes that where he lived in

---

3　*A Booklet of Essays, Appreciations, and Annotations Pertaining to the Anthology of Amer-ican Folk Music Edited by Harry Smith*, p. 30. Washington, D.C.: Smithsonian Folkways, 1997. (Booklet included in the *Anthology of American Folk Music*.)

Hanover, New Hampshire, in 1998, the only person he knew of who spoke an authentic, chewy, old New England accent, full of "Ayuh" and all the rest, was Walt the carpenter from across the river in Vermont, who "looks to be about 112 years old"—and not coincidentally, that "thirty years ago, three-quarters of the people in Vermont were born there. Today the proportion has fallen to barely half, and in some places it is much lower." Enough outsiders moved into Norwich, Vermont, that the old pronunciation "Norritch" was lost and it's now pronounced as an outsider would read it off a sign, "Nor-witch."[4]

In any case, the stasis of the language probably has a lot to do with the exact sorts of things that are likely to go away as the industrial tide recedes. The genesis of new accents will take a while—it takes a while under the most favorable conditions—but when TV blares its last commercial and radio becomes the preserve of a few hams per town, the American continent will be back on its way to becoming a patchwork of accents as rich as Britain, a place where a day's walk down an old trail might pass you through two or three distinct accents, and some of the most out-of-the-way places harbor accents so divergent as to be about impenetrable.

Now, picturing that scene, it's easy at least for a Statesider to imagine that everyone will revert to old accents full of folksy sayings that would sound at home in *Huckleberry Finn*. Here in the epicenter of the catastrophe of modernity, we really don't have much experience with accents outside the mainstream, aside from a few accepted variants like country-music Texan or Woody Allen New Yorker, and so imagining a patchwork of new Englishes sends us after our vague memories of Twain and Irving. We needn't go so far afield. To see where English is headed, just look to the teenagers.

It's a sobering thought, I know. But among linguists it's a well-accepted rule that if you want to find out where a language has been, you go talk to non-mobile, older, rural males—NORMs—and if you want to find out where it's going, you find teenage girls. Now, I can give you one sigh of relief in this, and it's that most slang words are ephemeral. So the odds that your grandchildren will still be saying, with a straight face, things like "He was on fleek" and "*Mood, breh*" are about on par with the chances for a revival of "Get jiggy with it" and "Talk to the hand." (It's the rare word that has the staying power of *cool*.) More than one author has fallen into the trap of putting old words into future mouths—the old-fashioned dialect of James Howard Kunstler's *World Made by Hand* books is a clear case, but even the masterful David Mitchell gave his Hawaiian future-English in *Cloud Atlas* a somewhat implausible *yay* and *nay*.

New grammatical patterns, though, new ways of slurring or replacing words—things like these are the changes that last after the slang fades, and

---

4   *I'm a Stranger Here Myself*, p. 94. New York, N.Y.: Broadway Books, 1999.

they start with young people. Young people were the ones who created "tryna" out of "trying to," with a meaning that's not quite the same. A new modal verb doesn't show up just every day; it's a real accomplishment for one to gain as much currency as this one has, and to me it looks like it has legs. (Clint Spivey in this issue appears to agree, as you'll see.) Equally, the accents—the spin of a vowel, the way one consonant swallows another—will start with young people. Will *mist* and *mists* both end up sounding like *miss*? Will *feel* start to sound like *fill* outside of urban centers? We'll have to wait and see. By then the rest of us will be old, and we'll be left to live in the weird-sounding speech-world they create.

Which brings me to a point that bears clarifying. When you're old and the bizarre-ass speech of young people has taken over your world, the natural reaction is to get at least a bit grumpy, if not fearful for the state of the world, and to say that everything is going down the crapper, because just look at the language and how it's degrading. Now, it's true that some changes in language do come from the weakening of sounds. That's why Germans say *weiss*; in this case English has been dowdier and sticks with *white* and its hard *t*.[5] But it's equally true that this doesn't amount to degradation. If people kept slurring their words more and more with each generation, with no countervailing tendency somewhere, then by now we would all be speaking in a sort of warbly groan—I hope you're with me if I mention the guy in *Hot Fuzz* who chopped down a hedge, whose dialog I would try to transcribe here if it had any intelligible sounds in it.

Of course languages don't "wear out." Among other things, that would imply that the first humans to speak did so in an impossibly complicated language, from which it has been downhill ever since. (Sorry, five-thousandth-great-grandma Qhñōʀāàçt, you invented language and we let you down.) In English, in fact, the words *six*, *apple*, and *gold*, among many others, are pronounced almost exactly as they were a thousand years ago. In general, languages have an interesting tendency to always be roughly equally complicated. When one thing vanishes, another comes in to replace it. In the Southern U.S., *pen* and *pin* have come to sound exactly the same for many people—and so these people now differentiate them by calling one an *ink pen*. As soon as language stops being useful for communication, people patch it up until it's useful again. John McWhorter argues that, left to their own devices, languages will actually tend to get gradually more complicated over time, until something happens to them.[6]

And that's where we get the entrance of the other important driver of language change that I haven't touched on: the historical curveballs. As much as

---

5 You can hear this exact same transition happening to English in real time, though, in a lot of Irish accents.
6 *What Language Is*. New York, N.Y.: Avery, 2012.

language can change all on its own, there's nothing like a massive historical shift to change things up. In 1389 the Lord's Prayer sounded like this:

Oure fadir
That art in hevenes
Halwid be thi name.
Thi kingdom come to
Be thi wille don
On erthe as in hevenes.

A little funky, but recognizable. That was 633 years ago; just 394 years before that, in A.D. 995, it looked like this:

Fæder ūre
Þū þē eart on heofonum
Sī þīn nama gehālgod.
Tō becume þīn rice
Gewurþe þīn willa
On erðon swā swā on heofonum.

What in heofonum happened? Well, some people had a fracas in 1066 and French-speaking armies took over England, killing or exiling the existing elites and imposing their language as the language of governance. Once the new order was accepted, people who wanted to be upwardly mobile learned French, imperfectly, and the French ruling class started peppering their speech with imperfect English, and eventually the language's grammar became vastly simplified as a result of so much upheaval. The Lord's Prayer doesn't even show a big chunk of the story: Before the Norman Conquest, English had a small scattering of loanwords from Latin, Greek, and other places, but was mostly pure Old English. Since Hastings, English has appropriated thousands—dozens of thousands, in fact, or even hundreds of thousands—of words from French and Latin. They make up half our dictionary now, and they're so much a part of English that we can't imagine the language without them. Just in that last sentence, I don't know how I would've done without *part, imagine,* and *language.*

Other languages have absorbed words and grammar from various unlikely sources. Spanish looks like a straightforward descendant of Latin, except for its liberal dusting of Arabic words from the Moorish era. Korea and Japan were so much under the sway of the Chinese imperial center in eras gone by that both their languages still have thousands of Chinese loanwords—pronounced, in many cases, more like the Middle Chinese source than the modern Mandarin version is — and more strangely still, they both maintain Chinese numbers along-side their own, native numbers, using the two sets to count different things.[7] The Métis, a French-Ojibwe mixed culture that arose in what's now Canada, developed a language called Michif that uses Ojibwe and Cree for the verbs but French for most nouns. English, then, as the imperial powers sustaining it wane and others begin to overtake them, could go in a hard-to-fathom number of directions.

All of which raises another interesting question. Aside from the question of what English will sound like, what about its place in the world?

Right now there are over a dozen countries in which English is spoken from birth by at least half a million people, and worldwide there are over 400 million first-language speakers of English. It's the most commonly learned second language in the world, and serves as a spoken lingua franca in at least 37 countries. Over three-quarters of the world's scientific papers are written in it, as is nearly a hundred percent of its computer code. Native English-speakers can find decent-paying language-teaching jobs in countries around the world based on almost no other qualification than having been raised English-speaking.

In other words, there's not much of anywhere to go but down.

Whether this means that countries that are currently English-speaking will get taken conquered, or whether it just means that an American will no longer be able to go to Norway without studying one scintilla of Norwegian first, there will almost certainly be a fall of English's star. And that's okay. The homogenization of communication has been taking place not just within English, but across the world as well. English supplanted over 500 Native languages when the U.S. and Canada took over this continent, and has done similar things in Australia, South Africa, New Zealand, Ireland, Scotland, Wales, and others. Many of these languages are gone for good. Some may stage a comeback. Welsh has a good chance, and Diné (Navajo) has more speakers now than it did before colonization.

Where English does survive, it will, in enough centuries, evolve into its own daughter languages: just as Latin developed into French, Spanish, Portuguese, Romanian, and the rest of their family, English looks very likely to become a set of similar but not mutually understandable languages across several wide and discontiguous areas.

A different detail is how long English will maintain its status as the world's lingua franca. Perhaps frustratingly, this is just as much up to historical contingency as the small details of phonemes and grammar are. English could lose its status as the world's "reserve language" almost overnight, or it could cling

---

7   For instance, when telling time in Korean, the hour is in Korean and the minute in Sino-Korean.

to the position of academic language for centuries, the way Latin did. There is something picturesque about the image of scholars in the far future sending each other articles in an English that approximates what we speak today, long after the countries that now speak it have ceased being political entities and the language hasn't been spoken in hundreds of years, unless you count its dozen or two offspring, all of which are so different from the original that even their literate speakers wouldn't be able to wade through a passage of Classical English. But that doesn't make it the guaranteed outcome by any means; a few wars in the right places and English could easily become a little-regarded regional language, just as Greek, once the medium of every philosopher who was anyone, is now — much changed — just another language along the Mediterranean coast.[8]

All of this is unknowable in advance. All possibilities, though, make interesting furnishings for stories, and help us imagine different ways the world could go from the present day.

Of course, not all these aspects of language will have a place in any one story. In fact most stories set in the future, including most in *New Maps*, are written in unmodified English. And that is fine. Even when a story is set centuries hence in a time that would certainly be host to a different version of English, it makes perfect sense to present that story in translation, as it were, rather than have the reader puzzle through a thicket of neologisms. One story clearly written in translation is John Michael Greer's *Star's Reach*: we see the English of the 25th century in placenames — Detroit has become Troy; Bloomington, Melumi — and in the names of the characters themselves, including the protagonist Trey sunna Gwen. Trey can read, but is flummoxed when another character writes a passage of English in the style of the 21st century, which is still used by haughty people on formal occasions. Often it's no more futurese than a glimpse like this that's required, if any is.

But in some stories, it just seems right to go whole-hog. Sometimes it's important to show that the culture has changed in some drastic way. *A Clockwork Orange* wouldn't be *A Clockwork Orange* without the Nadsat slanguage and the air of florid yet savage menace it projects. Other times it just has to be that way. *Cloud Atlas* presents six different time periods from the mid-1800s up to some unspecified year centuries from now. Mitchell tells each of the past sections in language carefully tuned to its day, and so naturally he must invent future English too. Though one gets the picture that he also just felt like it, which is another excellent reason to do it.

So let's say you're an enterprising author interested in inventing some future

---

8 Stories in this magazine have gone both directions: Daniel Crawford's "The Middle Sea" (iss. 2:1) has English fade quickly, while Wesley Stine's "Essential Services" (iss. 1:4) has it preserved as a lingua franca.

language of your own. How do you start? Despite all this discussion, you don't need a degree in linguistics, although it couldn't hurt to acquire one real quick if convenient. Here's the easy method.

First you want to decide what present-day dialect yours will be starting out as: obviously if you age Australian English by a few centuries, you'll get something different than if you started with Texan English. Now, inspect your dialect for what it does differently from others: does it bend its vowels funny so that, say, *out* becomes *ayowt*? Does it allow double modals like *might could*? And now start exaggerating. Bend those vowels even more; if they start sounding like another vowel, consider also bending that one away from it. If there are just a few double modals now, let them happen all the time: *could will* for speculations, *useta would* for reminiscences. And just have fun.

You get out what you put in. Close attention is rewarded. I've noticed signs lately saying EMPLOYEES MUST HAND WASH. Has *hand* become part of the verb? If you did it again, would you re-hand-wash? In a century, will people also dish-wash, nose-pick, horse-mount, and joke-tell? Or this: In many parts of England, an *l* at the end of a word is now pronounced as a *w*. ("For reaw?") What if the same thing happens there that happened in French when *nouvel* evolved through that phase into *nouveau*? ("I've got to toe you summink . . .") Any bit of language usage that strikes you as weird can be spun into a whole new feature of future speech. For those wishing to really nerd it up and go the extra mile linguistically, I can't strongly enough recommend recreational language inventor Justin B. Rye's article "Futurese,"[9] which imagines the progress of American English through a thousand years of upcoming history, with waypoints at A.D. 2100, 2400, 2700, and 3000.

Applying these rules will lead you to create a dialect that may sound ridiculous, maybe impossible to take seriously. But the tricky thing about English is that it's a language with few living relatives. So, while many Spanish-speakers will have seen bits of Catalan, Galician, and Aragonese, and will be familiar with "similar but different," the closest a lot of English-speakers will have gotten to that experience is while trying to puzzle out Shakespeare. Anything that isn't Shakespeare (or, possibly, Robert Burns) might appear childish. G. Kay Bishop, in the first issue of *New Maps*, started her story "Characters Written in Blood and Milk" audaciously with this:

> Aldest ya-zo daien dis daium: shee gibbewey mee er bootch. Gahst-ling bootch! Dey doo vum da Nugguzzun a da Nortlek-an. All Gadi-

9   In full, "Futurese: The American Language in 3000 AD." The JBR Home Page. jbr.me.uk/futurese.html

shilluns habun sunkaina nugguzzun ya-baiumbai. . . .[10]

It might seem goofy, but real life provides plenty examples of similar weirdness, like Jamaican singer Sean Paul's #1 hit from 2005, "Temperature":

> Bumper exposed and gyal, ya got your chest out
> But you no wasters 'cause gyal, ya impress out (Oh-oh)
> And if ya diss out a me, ya fi test out
> 'Cause I got the remedy fi make ya de-stress out (Oh-oh)

Or this snippet of an old Manitoba dialect called Bungi:

> John James Corrigal and Willie George Linklater were sootin the marse. The canoe went apeechequanee. The watter was sallow watefer, but Willie George kept bobbin up and down callin "O Lard save me." John James was on topside the canoe souted to Willie and sayed, "Never min the Lard just now, Willie, grab for the willows."[11]

Devising a form of language that unseats the reader from the familiar like this is a gutsy move, and it's not surprising that most authors who do it only give the language in little snippets, rather than sustaining it for a whole narrative. But in any case, it can't be counted as just superficial set dressing. When the very language keeps throwing curveballs at us, we piece together, at a level close to unconscious, that we are in an unfamiliar world whose rules, whose values and concepts, are all different. It helps us remember that the future we're heading into won't just be more of the same, a place where we can feel automatically comfortable. The future is a foreign country that we're all bound irrevocably to explore. We'd do well to keep our minds nimble for the journey: and so we look out for new meanings, new understandings, in each present day.

---

10 Which her character, forced to work in a scriptorium, translates laboriously as: "Eldest now-sure (yes, indeed?) dying this time: she gave me her boots. Costly boots! They two are from the No-Go-Zone of the North Lake (clan? -land?). All Goddess's children have them some kind of No-Go-Zone, now-by-and-by (now and forever)."

11 "Red River Dialect." *Winnipeg Evening Tribune*, Dec. 29, 1937. `digitalcollections.lib.umanitoba.ca/islandora/object/uofm%3A1829294`

Field Notes

Field Notes collects readers' accounts of notable landmarks the world is in the process of passing on its way toward the deindustrial age, and illuminating evidence of its progress down that path. Submit your story, observation, or other notes by emailing editor@new-maps.com; *please include "Field Notes" somewhere in the subject of your email.*

TRAIN CARS SIDELINED FOR YEARS

This is a small section of the miles and miles of train cars that have stood along U.S. Route 63 outside Spooner, Wisconsin, for at least five years. They are now more or less a landscape feature. The first mile or so are tank cars (I didn't get close enough to read what chemical(s) they're for); further on are several miles of grain cars. I've been unable to find information on when or why they were parked there, but I have a hard time interpreting their idleness there as a *good* sign for the industrial economy. Is that much less grain flowing through the country now? Did that many short line railroads get abandoned and cause small-town ag co-ops to have to pay stiffer rates to get fleets of trucks to empty their elevators? One thing that's certain is that this stretch of the Wisconsin Great Northern isn't moving stuff anymore. Will these train cars actually move if and when they're claimed? Might they still be there in a hundred years, too big for the local scrappers to make a dent in?

Nathanael Bonnell

More Midwestern decay

Ann Troxel sends in more photos of urban decay in the U.S.'s Midwest. She notes, "Passing through Muncie last time was especially eerie. Huge swaths of it are entirely abandoned."

STORIES

Pierre Magdelaine

The Mythmaker's Daughter

T HE PETRELS FLOATED on the wind with disconcerting ease, cawing and wheeling in the sky while waiting for their chance, wheeling and cawing, wheeling and cawing . . . and dropping like rocks to pierce through the water in a plume of white foam. They resurfaced a moment later, wriggling mackerels in their beaks, and floated peacefully on the waves for a while before swooping back up for another run.

Mary watched them from the stern of her sailboat with her fishing line in her hand and her long black hair flapping in the breeze. Every time a bird took flight her spirit rose with it into the blue. A gentle wind rose and filled the boat's sails. Mary's heart swelled with them at the sight of the expanse of waves and sunlight before shrinking back, dragged by the undertow: she imagined the shadow of a storm on the horizon, remembered how far they were from the coast, and her fears jutted out like so many reefs revealed by the ebb tide.

She felt a tug on her line and pulled in a large mackerel. The lively fish flailed energetically in her hands, its iridescent body shimmering in the sunlight. She dropped it in a crate and ambled over to the bow to wake up her daughter. Lyssa was lying on her side with her head reposing on her outstretched arm, her hand dangling over the side of the boat as if to greet some passing fish or seabird. The pressure of her shoulder against her cheek gave her small, thin-lipped mouth a sort of jaded pout she never wore when she was awake. Mary sat next to her. The girl looked so peaceful—more peaceful than Mary had been in a long while.

31

She and Lyssa had only seen smooth sailing so far, and they would be turning back soon, but Mary knew the sea: disaster could strike at any time. The wind could turn ... her daughter could fall overboard ...

She pushed away a strand of her daughter's hair that had fallen over her mouth.

"Lyssa," she said, shaking her gently by the shoulder. "Lyssa, wake up."

The girl opened her eyes and looked around her sleepily. How young and fragile she looked! A wave could crash on the deck and wash her away before Mary could do anything ...

"Time to prepare dinner, love."

Evening was slowly crawling up in the east, a cold shadow emerging from the darkening sea. Lyssa rubbed her eyes, gave a sharp nod, and pulled herself up, already wide awake. She made for the cabin, dancing adroitly against the pitching of the boat, and Mary's heart swelled again.

"In the beginning, the whole world was one giant ocean," Mary started, putting down her empty bowl beside her. The boat was gently rocking on the twilit waves; the sky, striped with long dark clouds, had turned a dusky shade of indigo. "The sea waters teemed with fish and shellfish, and the sky was filled with thousands of birds, but our ancestors, the first humans, despaired, because they had no land to rest upon.

"Among them lived a wise sorceress, who had learned the language of beasts. One day, she called into the sea for the gigantic beasts who lived there:

" 'Sister Turtle! Brothers Shark and Sturgeon!'

"The beasts swam up to the surface: the fish were as large as mountains, and Turtle vast like a continent. The sorceress asked them to stay at the surface of the ocean, so that her brethren could live on their backs.

" 'If we allow your kind on our backs,' Turtle answered, 'they will prosper and multiply until, one day, we won't be enough for them.'

"But the sorceress kept pleading; she told her about her people's misery as they wandered across the waters without a home, and, in the end, the giant beasts were convinced. They made an alliance with the sorceress:

" 'As long as your kind treat us with respect,' they promised, 'we shall give them a home.' "

The sky was darkening as Mary spoke, and the fading light of dusk drained out from the west. Lyssa too had finished her soup and was now scrubbing the bowls and cutlery in sea water. Mary lit the storm lamp and set it between them; its bright flame cast flickering shadows on her daughter's face and sparkled in her eyes.

"The sorceress' people, who had been scattered across the ocean, came to settle on the giant beasts, but they realized they could not live directly on their shells and scales, which were cold and slippery.

" 'We need soil,' they said: 'soil to plan trees and crops in, soil to build our houses on.'

"So the sorceress turned to the sky and called again:

" 'Sister Gull! Brothers Albatross and Cormorant!'

"And the birds came down to talk to her. She asked them if they were happy; they said they too needed land to rest and to lay their eggs. The sorceress asked them if they would dive to the bottom of the ocean to bring back soil to put on the beasts' backs.

" 'Very well,' said Gull, 'I will go.'

"She dove into the sea, but only half-way down she ran out of air and swam back up.

" 'You are not strong enough,' Albatross said. 'Let me go next.'

"He dove and swam for a long time, to the ocean floor, and he grabbed some soil, but when he came back to the surface all the soil had fallen from his beak.

" 'No, that's not how you do it,' said Cormorant, 'let me show you.'

"He dove down and reached the bottom of the ocean. He filled his beak with soil and swam back to the surface, and spit back the soil upon Turtle's shell."

The sea was completely dark now, the light from the storm lamp a quivering flame on the black waves. Lyssa sat cross-legged across her mother, nodding and swaying like a banner.

"Then the sorceress sang a magic spell," Mary went on, "and the soil Cormorant had spat spread over Turtle's shell, and Gull and Albatross took some over to the giant fishes' backs, and as the sorceress kept singing, plants appeared: first grasses and flowers, then bushes and trees, and so the islands and the continents were born."

Mary carried her daughter into the cabin, where she put her to bed with a kiss on her brow, and came back out to sit cross-legged at the bow, with the lamp at her back shooting her long shadow onto the waters like an arrow. She bowed and prayed:

"Mother Ocean, please carry our prow onto your breast,
  devour us not in wrath;
  please keep my daughter safe."

Every night Mary prayed, and every night she reminded herself she did not really believe in any of it; still she looked out into the darkness and repeated the words as if, were it not for their magic, the sun would not rise the next day and drive out the night.

> "Brother Wind, please guide our sails to plenty,
>   strike us not with storms;
>   please keep my daughter safe."

The words calmed her. The sea was the dominion of fears, which circled her like sharks—fear for her supplies, fear for the boat, and most of all fear for her daughter ... Everything was dangerous here: sleeping was dangerous, lack of sleep could be even more dangerous.

> "Sister Sky, please watch over our boat,
>   light the stars to guide us;
>   please keep my daughter safe."

Maybe she should have left Lyssa on the shore, and maybe even stayed there with her ... like every time she wondered what her husband would have thought, her grief rose like a wave to drown her. "When will you be back, petrel?" came the echo of his voice. He'd liked to joke that, like the seabird, Mary only came ashore to mate. He'd come from the hinterland, and the shore had always been the end of his world: it was he who had sewn trees on the boat's sails and carved mountains on the hull—to remind Mary, he'd say, what she must always come back to. Mary ran her fingers across the sea-sprayed prow. The marks in the wood were starting to fade; she wondered if the pain would fade as well, with time.

Mary pulled on the line to bring in another mackerel and thought: That's the last one for today.

The night had passed with no incident; she'd woken up Lyssa just before dawn and they'd followed the seabirds to their fishing grounds. They had spent the day sitting at the stern, their lines in hand, listening to the waves and the wind ... the sea, Mary had found, had a way to teach silence even to the most unrepentant windbags, and neither of them had ever been very talkative.

Now the afternoon was drawing late and Lyssa had abandoned her post to sit at the bow and watch the waves with the thoughtful look she'd inherited from her father, her black ponytail floating in the wind. Mary remembered the old ballad her husband used to sing to her: "Black, black, black, is the color of my true love's hair ..." She dropped the thrashing mackerel in the crate with the rest of the day's catch and looked up at the sky before the boat, where thick gray clouds were starting to assemble in the distance.

"Mom ... I think there's something over there."

Mary put away her line and walked over to her daughter. Lyssa was pointing to a dark spot on the horizon, in front of the boat, slightly to starboard. There was definitely something out there, but it was too far to make out. Mary went to get her binoculars.

"It's a wreck!"

"Let me see, let me see!" Lyssa said excitedly, wresting the binoculars from her mother's hands.

Something tightened in Mary's chest, and a cold foreboding crept inside her heart.

"Time to go back, love. Do you want to take the—"

"There's someone there!" Lyssa interrupted her. "Mom, there's someone in the debris, look!"

She handed the binoculars back to her mother and Mary looked again. Lyssa was right: there was a human shape slumped over a broken mast, its feet trailing in the water.

"We have to help them!" Lyssa exclaimed.

The coldness in Mary's chest spread to the rest of her body, seeping into her bones, making her blood turn to ice. She scanned the sea for a clue; she looked at her daughter's eager face and at the gray clouds over the horizon. They'd have to sail toward the storm, and they'd be taking a stranger with them on the boat ... But could they turn their backs on someone in need? someone whose life they had a chance to save? Mary's hesitations pitched with the boat.

"Mom?"

"Set the jib."

She crossed over to the wheel and took the boat under the wind. The sails filled with a snap and the boat jumped on the choppy water. "Grab on to the lifeline!" she ordered her daughter. Her heart started to beat faster, jumping from wave to wave with the boat while wind and fear whipped at her face; still she kept on course, glancing now and then at the clouds crouched menacingly on the horizon.

"Sir! Here, sir!" Lyssa cried when they were close enough.

The man slipped down from his broken mast and swam toward them. They helped him climb aboard—his arms, Mary noticed, were cold as death. He collapsed on the deck and coughed up water. Lyssa helped him sit up against the gunwale while Mary fetched freshwater. He drank and thanked her with a nod.

The castaway was tall, very gaunt, and pale. His narrow face was covered in a scraggly beard, turned gray and rigid by salt and dripping with seawater; he had black hollow eyes and wispy hair, his ribcage was visible under his tattered shirt ... in truth, Mary thought he looked more like a corpse than a man. He wore a silver chain around his neck and a small oilskin pouch on his belt. Mary caught a glimpse of a tattoo beneath the flaps of his shirt—something like a snake, coiled around an object she couldn't quite make out, inked across his protruding ribs. Her heart beat faster. For a reason she couldn't clearly make out, she was suddenly reminded of something her husband had told her years ago about cuckoo birds. "They're parasites," he'd explained. They'd been outside, behind the house—it was coming back to her in bits and pieces, like the debris of a wreck spat back by the deep and floating up to the surface of her memory— "They don't feed their own young, you see: they lay their eggs in the nests of other birds so they will feed the cuckoos' chicks in place of their own." He stitched as he spoke—mending her sails, maybe—while she sat in the slanting light of a quiet morning and listened: "The cuckoo birds always hatch first, and they grow faster, and because they're bigger and louder, they get more food than the other chicks." He was always so full of stories; myths and legends but also smaller stories like this. "And when they get big enough, they push the other chicks out of the nest."

"Centuries passed, and our ancestors forgot all about the sorceress' alliance and Turtle's warnings; they even forgot about the giant beasts on which they lived."

The darkening sky streaked with indigo and purple, Lyssa washing the dishes by the flickering light of the storm lamp, the boat dancing on the waves … it was evening again, the time for stories.

"They had built boats to fish and explore the world, and their empires soon spanned the continents and the seas, but they always wanted more: more wealth and more land, more than they would ever need, all because of a strange idea they called 'Justice.'" The castaway still hadn't said a word. He was barely a silhouette in the gloom, just on the edge of Mary's vision, but his silence seemed a physical thing, like a mantle of shadow giving him a more corporeal, tangible form. "Some, through force or craft, had grown wealthier than the others," Mary went on, trying to ignore him. "They said Justice meant they should have more, because they deserved it: they dug into the earth for riches, they turned the beasts' bones into metal and they burned their black blood for heat and power. But poorer people didn't agree, they said Justice meant they must get just as much as the rich; and so they must dig deeper into the giant beasts' flesh to find more metal and more oil, and to feed themselves as they claimed they deserved, they covered the lands with fields and cattle, and they ate, and ate, and ate … in fact, they grew more food than they could eat: what they didn't need, they threw away, filling giant fields with mounds of rotting waste. And as the poor got more the rich insisted they must have even more, and so they dug deeper still, and the poor in turn did as well to catch up, and the mounds of waste grew ever higher on the land … All in the name of Justice."

The sun had disappeared beneath the horizon; the wind sang in the rigging and whispered in the furled sails. Lyssa nodded, struggling hard to fight off her drowsiness. Not far astern, a mass of clouds banked the horizon in blackness.

"The waste decayed and poisoned the land; rain washed the filth into the rivers and then the ocean, where it fed toxic algae and killed the rest, the fish and the birds ... and this is why, though the waters of the world were once teeming with fish, we must now sail so far from the coast to find them.

"The beasts of the sea stirred in the poisoned waters, soured and warmed by the oil fires, causing storms and tidal waves with their writhing:

" 'They drill into our flesh and bones!' Sturgeon growled.

" 'They poison the waters and the land!' Shark raged.

" 'They've forgotten about us,' Turtle lamented.

" 'We should never have trusted them,' her brothers roared. 'They broke our alliance.'

"Turtle tried to stop them, but the giant fishes dove back into the depths, and the islands were lost to the sea; Turtle herself couldn't withstand the warmth of the surface and she swam a little deeper, and the coasts of the continents were submerged."

When she came back out of the cabin, Mary found the castaway sitting against the gunwale.

"Your daughter's name is Lisa?" he asked in a hoarse voice.

Mary started: she hadn't yet heard the man speak. "Lyssa," she corrected. She sat opposite him. "After the ancient Greeks' goddess of mad rage and frenzy," she explained with a half-smile. "When she was born, she cried with so much fury—we couldn't have imagined such a little thing could be so loud."

"She seems quieter now."

Mary nodded. The man's smile looked like a gash across his hollow face.

"You sure like your stories."

A cold hand clawed at Mary's heart. She passed her arm over the gunwale to touch the carvings on the hull.

"Her father did."

It was too dark now, even with the storm lamp, for Mary to make out the expression on the man's face. The night had swallowed his shirt and his strange tattoo; he was nothing now but a pair of black eyes, a breath, and a low, raspy voice that seemed to come from the grave:

"I'm sorry. Is that why you took her with you?"

Mary looked out to the black clouds at their back, which seemed to be running after them, out from the darkness. She was so tired, so scared, and so tired of being scared ... Fear and weariness had submerged her world and her thoughts swam like minnows in their waters, one darting away chased by another, by a splash, a yaw, a bird's cry—nothing now but a trail in the water … soon it was gone, and only the ocean of fear and weariness was left.

"There's no one left landside to take care of her. Her father … he was fascinated by old myths and legends, he knew so many of them … he told one to her every night and she could never get enough of them—stories filled with heroes and monsters and cruel gods … And now …" Mary's hand tensed on the carved hull. "I don't know those stories, so I try to make up some new ones for her, so that she …"

She hung her head. The man had closed his eyes.

"That's alright," he said. "We need new stories."

The storm overtook them the next day. Just after midday, the sun disappeared into a mass of thick, dark, gunmetal clouds and the wind, which had been rising gradually since morning, suddenly picked up. The boat rocked on the roiling waves, and its sails cracked in the sudden gale.

"Set the storm jib," Mary ordered her daughter, and to the castaway: "Get inside." She looked indecisively at her compass and at the clouds, while large waves heaved under the boat and made it pitch threateningly, forcing her to grab on to the pulpit; rain pattered on the sails—"Inside, now!" she cried to Lyssa. The boat gave a sudden yaw that almost threw her overboard.

"Brother Wind," she breathed, grabbing at the wheel, "please strike us not in wrath."

The petrels were back, their piercing cries a welcome relief after hours of crashing waves and howling winds. Lying on her back in the stern, her muscles sore and her mind weary, Mary looked down from the wheeling birds to her daughter. Her clear brown eyes, shielded from the evening sun by the visor of her white cap, were fixed on the blue horizon with a tense concentration. The wind had torn a strand of black hair from her ponytail; it waved before her face as if to point her in the right direction.

"Black, black, black, is the color of my true love's hair," Mary sang,

"Her lips are something wondrous fair,

She's a wonder and well she knows

I love even her snotty nose."

The shadow of a smile passed on Lyssa's lips. She had not said a word since she'd come out of the cabin an hour ago and her mother asked her to take her place.

"We'll be alright, love."

The girl nodded. Mary sat up against the stern pulpit and looked across the boat.

"The mast and sails are fine and we caught a good tail wind. If it holds, we'll be back home in three days."

"But ..." Lyssa said, finally breaking her silence, her small voice and black ponytail flailing in the strong wind, "what about the fish?"

Mary looked at her uncomprehendingly for a moment, and then all the tension that had built up in her chest went out in a burst of laughter. "Don't worry about the fish. We lost a crate, that's nothing."

Lyssa loosened slightly and answered her mother's smile. For all Mary had tried to teach her, she was still a landside girl: she never had had to go without freshwater, so she couldn't guess at the anguish tugging at her mother's heart.

The castaway emerged from the cabin and walked nimbly to the bow. Mary stood, patted her daughter on the head, and joined him. Though still just as pale, the man seemed changed — there was something like an increased sense of presence to him, as if the storm had breathed life into his cadaverous body.

"You never told us what happened to your boat."

"A storm. Two storms in three days ... I must be cursed," the man added, with a bitter smile.

"What about your companions?"

He kept his eyes on the sea. The sun, suspended before the boat like a beacon, bathed the man's pallid face in a ruddy light.

"I'm sorry."

The petrels wheeled and cried above them.

"What were you doing out there?"

His eyes were cold and hard like stones.

"Fishing," he said, after a spell. "We were fishing."

His open shirt floated like a shroud on his hollow chest. The evening light fell between the tattered flaps on the large black tattoo — "there's a black eel stitched on their sail, coiled around a fish hook" — the memory suddenly resurfaced in Mary's mind, and the fear that had been sleeping there swelled like a wave: the damp evening, fishermen and sea-merchants gathered around the ruddy stove in the house where sailors met, "—three ships attacked, and that's only those they let go ..." — the voice of a merchant from a city up north on the coast; Mary knew him well, he'd always been a bit of a fabulist but this time he was truly scared, everyone around the table had sensed it. They'd huddled closer to the stove, thinking of lost friends whose disappearance they'd chalked up to the storms ...

The castaway turned, caught Mary's look, and closed his shirt. Mary walked back to her daughter. When she sat back in the stern, the castaway had turned back to the horizon with a deep frown, as if in concerned deliberation.

"Are you alright?" Lyssa asked.

"Yes." Mary forced a smile. "Just a bit tired is all."

The castaway's mouth was set with determination and the evening had lit a sinister glint in his eyes.

The petrels were gone and the wind was dying; the boat was the last island of life on the silent sea. The castaway sat in the bow, watching Lyssa gaze distractedly at the waves. Mary, having hauled down the sails and furled them for the night, filled a basin with sea water to do the dishes, searching for a new story to tell, some optimistic, reassuring fairy tale, *"Once upon a time..."* —but the castaway's shadow was here, watching her daughter.

"Mom, look!" Lyssa exclaimed. "Eels!"

Mary put a bowl down and looked overboard into the waters, where eels were taking advantage of the darkness to come up to the surface.

"Do you know where they come from?" the castaway asked.

Mary looked up: the man had stolen close to her daughter and was looking into the water with her.

"Mom told me: they were born far into the sea, then they swam inland to grow in the lakes and river, and now they're swimming back to the deep sea to make babies."

"Mmh. And did your mother tell you that, sometimes, eels are not what they appear?"

Lyssa turned perplexedly to the castaway, then to her mother, and back to the pale man.

"What do you mean?"

"Sometimes, eels are not eels ... sometimes they're really ghosts, trapped between the sky and the deep, and they turn into eels to visit sailors on the line of the horizon, where the elements meet."

The rigging and the furled sails clicked and flapped in a light breeze, the waves breathed against the hull. Mary, her muscles and nerves taut, briefly looked up from her washing. The feverish flames in the castaway's eyes had died down, but they still gave a smoldering light, like embers a mere gust of wind could set alight.

"Do you want me to tell you the story of one of these ghosts?"

Lyssa nodded, already enthralled, and the shadow smiled.

"One day," he said, "a ship dropped anchor by a desert island. Its crew had been at sea for weeks, and they were about to run out of freshwater." Mary's hands clenched in the seawater basin. She licked her lips. The castaway did not spare her a look: his attention was entirely focused on her daughter. "The crewmen set across the island looking for water. After a few hours, they met an old sailor who told them he'd washed up there years ago, and that he would lead them to freshwater if they brought him with them when they left. They agreed, and he took them to a spring hidden deep in the island. He told them to wait for him on the shore." Mary gathered the dishes and took them in the cabin. Outside, the castaway's raspy voice kept on, floating on the waves' lapping: "When the crew came back with freshwater the captain, who'd stayed to watch the ship, asked them where they found it. They told him about the old man and the deal they'd made with him, but as soon as the water and all the crew was on the ship, the captain ordered they raised anchor immediately. The crewmen protested, reminding him of what they'd promised the old man.

"'No one lives on this island,' the captain answered. 'That isn't a man you saw, but a ghost.'"

Mary came out of the cabin. Lyssa sat enthralled, her eyes shining and her mouth agape, under the castaway's crooked shadow.

"The frightened sailors followed their captain's direction and sailed off. When the old man arrived on the beach, they had almost disappeared ... But the ghost ran to the sea and changed into a giant eel to chase them — the terrified crew tried to escape, but he caught up with them and capsized the ship —" the castaway looked up to Mary " — and cast them all into the deep."

Mary stopped dead. She and the castaway looked at each other in silence, Lyssa shivering between them. Mary clenched her teeth and felt her muscles tense with resolve. The man looked down at Lyssa.

"Some say the captain became a ghost himself, cursed to wander between sky and sea, night and day, life and death ... He haunts the waves, visiting unwary sailors who, like him, have ventured too far into the sea ..."

"Lyssa," Mary called, "time to turn in, love."

"But I want to hear the end of the story!"

"Oh, but this is it," the man said, turning back to Mary. "This is the end."

Mary took Lyssa by the shoulder and into the cabin. Moments later, the girl was sound asleep.

"Sister Sky," Mary prayed, looking on her peaceful face, "please keep my daughter safe."

The castaway had conjured a cigarette — an actual honest-to-god, orange-and-white, filtered cigarette — and was leaning close to the storm lamp to light it. Twilight was only a distant indigo line; they were alone on the dark expanse. He took a long drag and blew up a cloud of smoke.

"There's not enough freshwater left." There was a cold finality in his voice, as if he were a judge passing sentence. "My guess is we're at least five to six days away from land, and what's left won't last us more than two days. That leaves three to four days without freshwater ... You know this means death."

Mary shuddered.

"Not necessarily," she tried. "If we're very careful, if the winds are favorable ... if it rains ..."

"Enough!"

She recoiled as if from a whip.

"We're done for, and you know it." He went on, in a quieter voice: "Now, if there was only two of us ... they might have a chance. It would be hard, no doubt, but at least they'd have a chance."

Mary steeled herself for the fight: it wouldn't be long—any moment now he would stand and jump at her ... Why did he even trouble explaining himself? Was he so sure of his superiority that he didn't worry about letting her ready herself? Or did he feel he owed her an explanation because she saved his life? Because she had. She'd welcomed the cuckoo's egg into her nest, she'd even put it there herself. But though this knowledge weighed heavy in her heart, she knew she'd never had a choice. She couldn't have left him to drown. In the end, it must always come to this; the rocking boat, the flickering flame of the lamp, the dark waters and the star-strewn sky, the red dot at the end of his dying cigarette, and:

"There's only one solution."

He seemed so sad. Did he want her pity? Her forgiveness? Mary clasped her fingers firmly around the handle of the knife she'd secreted from the cabin and kept against her leg, in her own shadow, where the light of the lamp couldn't flash on the blade and betray its presence.

The man stood and flicked the extinguished cigarette overboard.

"Thank you," he said.

And he jumped into the sea.

Mary's knife clattered on the deck; she knocked over the storm lamp, grabbed the gunwale—there! his pale shape was swimming away into the blackness, his pallid arms lit by the cold starlight ... and then nothing: only the night and the sea, and between them Mary, shocked and confused.

The winds were kind to them: only five days later, Mary and her daughter saw the misty shape of land emerge from the sea like a giant beast. After a moment of doubt, Lyssa raced to the bow and cried:

"Land! Land!"

Mary looked fondly on her daughter, marveling at her energy. Those five days hadn't been easy: heat and exposure had harassed them constantly, nagging them with the temptation to drink just a little of the infinite sea—just a mouthful, just a drop—thirst dancing like a devil in their minds ... but Lyssa's spirit hadn't wavered. In their direst hours, when the burning sun was directly astride their boat and salt and wind glued their parched mouths shut, she'd only touch the braided silver chain on her neck and smile with a strange confidence.

"You know, mom, I'd guessed he was a ghost," she'd declared the morning after the castaway had disappeared.

"A ghost?"

Mary had been unsure what to say. How could she explain what the man had done? She hadn't slept; soon after the castaway had gone a favorable wind had picked up and she'd unfurled the sails to take advantage of it. Strange thoughts, muddled with doubt and gratitude, had floated in her mind throughout the night.

"The ghost of a castaway," Lyssa had insisted. "You know, in the story, the ghost sinks the ship because the sailors didn't keep their promise—but it's just like in dad's stories: when you cheat the spirits, they punish you; but if you help them, they reward you instead."

She'd opened her hands to show the castaway's silver chain and his oilskin pouch. Inside the pouch were a dozen shiny pearls and a cardboard pack of filtered cigarettes, with only one missing.

"But I guessed he was a ghost before he disappeared."

"Did you?"

"Of course. He was so pale, mom, and so sad ..."

Mary sat back against the stern pulpit. Gulls cried above the boat to welcome them home, and the rocky coast appeared more clearly through the mist. "Some say the captain became a ghost himself," the castaway's hoarse voice echoed through her memory, "cursed to wander between sky and sea, night and day, life and death ... He haunts the waves, visiting unwary sailors who, like him, have ventured too far into the sea ..." Mary smiled and watched her daughter grab the bow pulpit and stand on tiptoe as if to peer over the horizon, her ponytail flapping wildly in the wind, the silver chain shining like a beacon around her neck.

JJ Dettman

Greenland

T HE LONE BULB in the upper corner of the room flashed in long, authoritative pulses. Its light washed every surface in an unnatural red, then left behind total darkness. The mechanical bell below the bulb was much more panicked in its duty. Niels turned over beneath his covers, groaned, then pulled himself out of his bed and into his robe and slippers. What incredible volume for such a tiny device, he thought.

Niels was the last of his colleagues to get to the central work room. There were just three others, all standing in front of computer monitors, silhouetted against the blue-white of the screens. Someone had turned the alarms off. Niels flipped on the lights and dimmed them low.

Rasmus was at the helm. The cursor flipped from icon to icon, fanning their data out across the four monitors. One screen was dedicated to a full map of Greenland spotted with status markings for the team's research stations across the continent.

No one spoke as they each performed their own analysis. There were problems with two outflow stations in the southwest, that much was clear. The question was what kind. Either something new was happening to the Greenland ice, or their sensors had failed in a new way.

"This can wait until morning, yes?" Päivi said, breaking the minutes-long silence.

Rasmus leaned back in the big chair and bumped into Niels, who towered over the desk, the chair, everything — motionless, thin wisps of breath streaming from his pursed lips. They had seen this look of contemplative concern many times before.

Päivi leaned into Niels's view and said, "I know, it is strange, but if it was bad, we would see something else, don't think you think?" Päivi Hallamaa was the lone professor in the room, making her the de facto authority figure. Informally,

44

however, anyone committed enough to stay at Zackenberg over the winter — student or faculty — was considered an equal member of the team. "Let's sleep and come back in the morning."

Niels nodded. "Morning" was just a number on a clock at that time of year.

"I'd like to go out and see. Just to be sure," he said. "If that's alright."

Päivi buried her hands further into her arms. It was tough to keep Niels inside, even in the permanent dark of winter. The others waited. She shrugged, with a smirk, and said, "Okay."

"I will keep you company," Rasmus offered. He went off to make coffee, shivering, and reassured the others they could go back to bed. Marina, a recent addition to the group, covered herself with her blanket and shuffled down the hall. Propane grew increasingly scarce with every year, and heating was not the top priority in their energy budget.

Päivi stopped Niels before he hurried off. "Be safe," she said. Niels was her lone graduate student. Since the main camp had emptied out in September it'd been just the four of them at Zackenberg. Prof. Hallamaa preferred to keep her world small. It gave her fewer things to worry about. "You call us soon as you see something."

Niels nodded, and assured her he'd be back before she woke up.

Rasmus met Niels in the hangar and put a travel mug in the cockpit of their plane. He started spraying the wings with a de-icing solution by hand, taking his time. Half of Niels's wide, angular frame was already in the winter suit. The pants gave his legs the bulging appearance of over-packed sausage.

On a shelf against the wall sat a compact robotic device hardly bigger than a toaster. Rasmus unplugged it and tapped it twice on a head-like protrusion at the front. The appliance rose of its own accord, revealing four metallic legs curled beneath its body. It leapt to the floor, tested its joints with a few wiggles and squats, then stood still, head cocked at Rasmus. Dr. Hallamaa had spent an entire year's acquisition budget on the slightly used explorer drone. The scientists at Zackenberg named her Ludde. She was the closest thing to a pet for a thousand kilometers. Niels whistled and pointed at the rear of the cockpit. The robot hopped in and made itself comfortable.

After a final run through the take-off checklist, Niels shot his friend a nod, then climbed into the pilot's seat. Rasmus scampered back into the warmer indoor air, holding his steaming travel mug close.

Niels leaned back and pulled forward pleasant memories — holidays with his cousins; dark, hearty beers by the fireplace — and solidified them in the present with long, slow breaths. Once he found peace, he unwound the control cable from the dashboard and plugged it into the port behind his ear. The lights went out. His entire body spasmed, his vision flickered with bursts of bright and dark spots, and every inch of his skin sizzled as if it were being broiled under the sun. Before he could scream the worst of it passed. This was the price owed. His reward was total control. As if it were one of his arms, he lowered the cockpit door, then locked himself within as if clenching his fists. He called on the main generator, and the thrusters hummed to life. No bodily analogy could account for this, for the sensation of a hundred thousand horsepower fusing to your skeleton, within the fibers of your muscles, all ready to explode at the end of your thoughts. Niels had gone out in their ancient hand-me-down plane dozens of times. Despite the shock, he never grew tired of it.

He flipped on the comms. "Ready to go, Ras."

There was a warning buzz, then a thunderous rattling as the hangar door was heaved aside. The outdoor lights shone onto frozen piles of snow. Beyond, the infinite darkness beckoned. Niels pushed off with the vertical thrusters and eased his way out. The air was still and barely registered his presence. In a blink he was up and away, coasting at a third the speed of sound.

The sky was patchy with stretched, partially lit clouds, gesturing to where a half-moon intermittently showed its face. The snow-covered surfaces of the Earth glowed with an even cadence interrupted only by the sharp crags that punched through the thinner coastal ice. Before long, Niels left the Greenland sea behind and was out over the interior of the vast ice sheet. In winter, there were no surface rivers or lakes—no blemishes at all—and everywhere the snow fell level, so that from a thousand meters high, it looked as though a freshly laundered bedsheet had been pulled tight across the entire planet.

Rasmus read out loud the BBC's latest international headlines, some with a mocking tone. Niels and Rasmus kept their political discourse to themselves. Their colleagues preferred to stay out of the news, specifically that concerning the arctic, because most of it was trouble, and all of it was out of their hands. The far north had become the trendiest battleground for testing the limits 21st-century diplomacy. Stand-offs with hundreds of navy ships off the coast of Alaska, open threats involving intercontinental missiles in the evening news. Multi-billion-dollar games of chicken to determine whose name was fixed to the untapped reserves of arctic oil, and who got to charge admittance to international trading routes once covered with ice. All things considered, the scientists at Zackenberg viewed their governments as violent, impulsive third parties rather than true allies or adversaries. With one hand, these governments funded their work in combating climate change, and with the other, they fought amongst themselves with the same attitude and objectives that had jeopardized the global environment in the first place. For civilians, ignoring international politics provided mental relief at a time when that was difficult to find.

"Rasmus, there's something here," Niels said, interrupting. He brought the seat forward so he could inspect the ground. He slowed the plane to a hover.

In the middle of the infinite white there was a splotch. The ice here was over a kilometer thick. No chance it was a mountain peak.

"Can you check my coordinates—" Niels dictated the latitude and longitude from his GPS.

"The radar says the same," Rasmus confirmed. He checked all their maps. "There is supposed to be nothing. What do you see?"

"Not sure. Just a dark mess." Niels began stuffing himself into his dense winter gear. "I'm going down."

"Should I wake up the others?"

"Not yet."

The plane jostled onto the ice. Niels flinched and disconnected the control cable, then opened the door with his hands.

The air was shockingly still. The cold scraped Niels's cheeks, which were the only exposed part of his skin. The moon slipped behind a cloud and Niels lost his target in the total darkness. He switched on his headlamp and red light spilled onto the dry, packed snow.

It was a scene of destruction. The scattered, exploded remains of a compact building. Thick sheets of galvanized steel crumpled like paper. It was impossible to tell what exactly had been inside. Everything was coated in soot and scorch marks or half-buried in snow. The remains of a bed, some computers, communications equipment, a charred sleeping bag, the bottom shell of an exploded propane tank. Taking a closer look at the arrangement of the chaos, Niels concluded the tank had clearly exploded after whatever else had blown a hole through two centimeters of steel.

There, a few meters from the tank. A jacket. Just the sleeve. An arm was still in it. No sign of the rest of the torso. Niels glanced at the debris. A body could easily be lost in there. He covered his mouth with his sleeve, then turned the arm over with the end of a hammer. There was no patch identifying who the limb had belonged to, or which worldly organization had given this jacket to them.

Niels turned away from the wind, pulled his gaiter down, and relayed the scene to Rasmus. By his guess, the shack had been standing no longer than a week ago.

Rasmus cursed in Swedish. "We have to call someone."

Niels didn't respond. Who? The military? Who says they weren't involved?

"Wait," Niels said. "Let me check our station first. I'm almost there."

"I don't like that, Niels."

"I will be fast."

Niels hurried back to the plane, plugged in with a shudder, and took off. He was close enough now to follow one of the pipes directly to the first station. The pipes were heated to five degrees to keep the water from freezing, so they stood out as a gray, sodden line of muck amongst the pristine snow field.

"Niels, what's going on?" Päivi's voice came into the comms—panicked, and unlike her. Niels tried to downplay the situation regarding the unidentifiable, unregistered, and recently exploded shack in the middle of the ice sheet. He hoped he sounded calm. He could feel his blood throbbing in his wrists against the tight glove straps.

"Can you ask Igloolik if they saw anything strange?" Niels said, moving the conversation somewhere else. He wasn't far now. Marina offered to check in with their colleagues.

In the distance, a familiar rectangular structure poked out of the snow. The lumpy line guiding Niels ended at one of the walls. He dove low with the plane and came to a sliding stop a hundred meters from the building. He grabbed his gear and tapped Ludde on the head.

A piercing breeze cut in from the west. The exposed rock of the coast wasn't far now. Niels pulled his hood over his hat, leaned into the wind, and trudged away from the plane. His snowshoes sank into the crunchy snow, which lifted off in the breeze like sand. Ludde unfurled a pair of wings inset with mechanical fans and hovered along behind him. Niels asked the drone to go ahead and scout a path. The ice at the fringes of the sheet was rotten, even in winter. Pits and crevices could hide anywhere beneath the thin, brittle surface. There was no danger if he was careful.

A snowdrift had buried the main entrance to the station. Niels pulled out the ladder, swapped his snowshoes for crampons, and climbed up onto the roof, which was made of the same galvanized steel that he'd seen torn to shreds a half-hour ago. He hacked through ice and pried the roof hatch open. He pulled the string for the lone bulb in the ceiling and a warm glow erased the darkness of the windowless space.

The room was tight. Not meant for long-term habitation. There were a couple computers clustered on one desk with a screen mounted on the wall. A drawer full of tools and sensors. Technology that was brand-new a decade ago. A hammock was folded neatly in the corner, not recently used. Niels had spent a few nights in one of those last summer. His breath hung in the air like thin miniature clouds.

Nothing was obviously amiss, just as their data at Zackenberg had said. In the back corner, a solid pipe as thick as Niels' wingspan came straight through the wall, bent ninety degrees, then disappeared into the floor, where it continued downward, boring through a half kilometer of ice until it reached the space where the ice sheet met solid rock.

This pipe, as with the other stations in the vast network monitored by the team at Zackenberg, was the focal point of their whole mission. Their job was to slow the ocean-bound motion of the Greenland ice sheet by extracting the melt water that ran underneath it. In some places the water collected into rivers that pushed the ice downhill, acting as a sort of lubricant. Once the ice broke off from the rest of the sheet and fell into the open ocean, it was doomed. However, if that meltwater were to be removed—say, pumped upwards, using the pressure from the massive weight of the ice to do most of the heavy lifting—then this motion would be slowed, and the melt rate reduced. As a bonus, the liquid water now at the top of the ice sheet could be redistributed along pre-existing faults to reseal them, if the weather was right. Their project began ten years prior and had immediate impact. Within a year, the melt rates in Greenland stabilized, for the first time in a century. The faltering North Atlantic Ocean currents recovered. It was a rare, albeit isolated, victory in humanity's struggle against itself, and the project became a symbol of hope. The pipes alone could not solve the numerous environmental threats related to climate change, but they did buy time, and the continued health of the second-largest mass of ice on Earth—and by extension most life on the planet—depended on how humanity used that extra time.

Niels inspected the pipe up close. Its surface was rough, bumpy, and un-painted. Like any tool designed to do a job first and appear presentable second. He put his ear to the metal, then, after hearing silence, opened a release valve, and nothing came out. It was time to figure out why.

Niels undid the twelve bolts pinning the chest-sized service hatch to the pipe, then heaved it onto the floor. The rusty smell of stale freshwater wafted out with it. Niels stuck his head in and looked down. Darkness stared back. Clicks, taps, and other grating sounds echoed up in an endless series of agitated bursts, like an argument destined to last forever. This was the ice adjusting and readjusting against the reinforced pipe, as if it were alive, and rejecting the intrusion that pierced its body. Niels supposed that, under similar circumstances, his body would react in the same way.

He let out one, short syllable: "*bøh*," to surprise anyone waiting down there. His voice echoed down the pipe until it faded away, and never came back.

"The pipe is completely dry," Niels said to his colleagues, taking his head out. "I am sending Ludde down to see more."

The drone was resting on the desk in its compact airborne shape, resem-bling an aluminum football with wings. Niels brought Ludde out of sleep, while holding down a button behind his own ear, set to the wireless pair function.

There was a brief prick, like a needle—barely noteworthy compared to the gross discomfort of the old plane—then Niels and his drone were connected. His mind streamed two visual feeds at once: one from his human eyes, and another from the sensors at the front of Ludde's body, which could perceive not just visual but also infrared and weakly ultraviolet light. As he held the drone in his hands, directed towards his face, there was an effect much like looking into a mirror, as the drone's beady lenses returned an image of his rosy, fleshy visage glowing gently against the dim arctic backdrop, which was some fifty degrees colder than his skin. It was to observe himself on the outside, but from within.

The effect gave inexperienced pilots heavy bouts of vertigo. But Niels and Ludde were well acquainted.

The drone's mechanical physiology was now at Niels's command. He willed Ludde into the pipe and began a descent into the abyss. Niels walked over and watched the small, delicate machine vanish from sight.

The front-facing LEDs illuminated the dark passage. There wasn't much to see; the same segments of pipe repeated themselves over and over. Lone jewels of water clung to the walls and sparkled in Ludde's light. The pipe was designed to be mildly flexible, and forfeit space to the advances of the ice where possible. This meant that the path to the bottom was not straight, and the fastest Niels could fall was a controlled, swinging descent at the pace of a light jog. White distance markers composed of circles and slashes marked his progress.

"I am at the bottom now, still no sign of standing water," Niels said with his eyes closed. The lips of the pipe were lined with jagged teeth.

Ludde slipped into the terminal cave. Niels put the drone in the classic quad-copter configuration, turned up all the LEDs, and gave himself a full, spherical view of the space.

He was surrounded by air. The scraped, rocky ground was exposed; barely a stream of melt trickled through. Just yesterday there had been so much water here that it could be piped up a kilometer against gravity and still have enough pressure left over to maintain a steady flow. And the cave had shrunk. Ludde hovered not even two meters from the bare rock. According to their records this cave was supposed to be three times that height.

Niels described the empty, misshapen cave to his colleagues while he went to the computer screens to look at data. Ludde hovered down below, waiting.

"I need all of you to look at the seismic activity," he said in a short burst. The seismometer measured mechanical vibrations in the ice, i.e. "icequakes." In the last twenty-four hours there were no standout events—no single spike big enough to trigger automatic warnings, or even raise concern when the full crew at Zackenberg had consulted this figure just a few hours prior. But they'd missed something. They'd been looking for broken limbs, blood clots, cardiac distress, and missed the patch of bruises, which presented here as an anomalously fre-quent series of miniature quakes. This could come from an innocent injury—like a bad fall, or an over-exerted muscle—but Niels feared something much more serious, like internal bleeding. Ten blips peeked over the background noise last night alone. It'd be strange to see more than one.

"Niels you have to get out," Rasmus said. "Right now." There were no re-buttals.

Niels turned Ludde over to its own piloting routines and activated the hom-ing beacon, maximum urgency. He arranged the bolts in an easily accessible row on the floor, stood the pipe hatch door at his side, and unclipped the swaying drill from his hip. He wasn't going to leave the drone behind. All he could do was wait for her. Snow skittered against the steel walls and roof; wind whistled through the grooves in the exterior wall, stopped, then started again. Niels tapped his boot on the padded floor. It brought him a sense of control against the noise.

There was a boom and a thousand cracks and then the ground leapt, tossing Niels against the wall. The world went quiet. Niels blinked. His vision was a blur. He could tell the walls were intact, so was the roof. The monitors had crashed to the floor. The pipe had buckled at the elbow, but mostly held its form. He tried one of his hands. It was intact. All of his limbs were attached correctly but the pipe hatch pinned his right leg to the ground. He couldn't tell how bad it was.

The room came back into focus. The fog lifted and he could hear his colleagues shouting into the comms. He had to turn down the volume.

"I'm okay," he said, then pushed the hatch off and went to stand up and fell right over. The leg was not okay. Touching the foot to the ground sent needles into his shin. No chance of even standing on it, but he could move. His arctic pants packed the leg tight. He hopped over to the ladder, leaning on the desk, then pulled himself up the ladder to the roof hatch.

The moon was out and the land glowed. Niels shuddered against the unimpeded wind. Not thirty meters from his compact shelter, a crater smoldered and simmered. Exploded chunks of ice surrounded the gaping hole. Finer ejecta sketched out a tail pointed downwind.

Another crash opened the sky. Niels ducked into the shelter and slammed the hatch.

"Cease fire!" he yelled, open to all frequencies. "I repeat: cease fire! Stop! I am a civilian! A scientist!"

Rasmus jumped on the radio and repeated the message in German, Marina in Russian and French.

There was no response.

Niels limped down from the ladder and rolled under the desk. Ludde hovered down beside him. He hadn't even noticed the drone's return. He wondered if she understood what was going on.

After a minute, no further explosions came. No reply, explanation, or apology. The whistling of the wind picked up again, as well as the gentle pattering of the airborne snow-ice tickling the steel walls.

"I am going to the plane," Niels announced.

"Be quick!" Päivi yelled.

He hurried out through the roof. On the ice, Ludde morphed into a bipedal form with extended limbs to give Niels a crutch. The moon came and went behind a series of clouds, concealing and then revealing the plane ahead of them. The crater from the second explosion was still simmering.

Niels stepped and his leg wobbled. His good one. If Ludde hadn't spun around to catch him he'd have fallen on his face.

The wobble came through again. It didn't come from his leg, but the ground. The ice was quiet. A gentle rumble crept in from the distance.

"*Hvad fanden var det*?" he said, peering into the empty, glassy eyes of the drone.

Another tremor, with a direction and purpose. Niels spun around. The snowy land had shrunk. Was shrinking. He could see the end of the world now, where white met black. It was closing in on him, with the roaring thunder of a tidal wave.

"*Gå!*"

Every step took the effort of a leap. The tremors grew faster, and harder, tossing Niels like the sea. The ice beneath their feet cried out in booming screeches and moans. Ludde tried to propel him forward but her thin arms lacked strength. Every time Niels got back up it seemed like the plane had moved farther away.

Then the floor vanished. Niels flew into the air while the ground fell to the center of the Earth, like a shelf had broken off the world. Gravity took over, and their fall commenced. The ice rushed up to meet them, and there was nothing Niels could do to stop it.

Total blackness, interrupted by fizzing lights streaking across the void, popping in and out of existence. A blanket of dull ringing from the inside. Vision returned, faded. Muddled patches of dark and white, chunk by chunk. Glistening sparks fell on his cheeks with a cool kiss. The floor rumbled against his body—calm, and regular, like he was shipping out on a great journey. Niels had always wanted to go to space.

There was a tug at his sleeve. A friend, the robot Ludde. It wanted him to grab something—a handle, something fixed in place, sturdy and unmoveable. He took hold and pulled himself forward because it felt like the right thing to do. The device directed him to another hold, and another, and then the floor become smooth, and level, and the rumbling stopped. The room was still. He'd arrived.

"Huh?" Niels shot up. He was lying on the floor of the plane. Ludde was curled up on the other side of the chair, watching him. They were in the sky, out over the great ice sheet, hovering in place. He grabbed on to the arm of the chair to pull himself up but then his brain throbbed against every inch of his skull and he had to stop. He gingerly took off his hood and his hat. An enormous welt ballooned off the left side of his head. No blood, but he could barely touch it. He rolled his way into the chair, then closed his eyes and waited for the wave of dizziness and throbbing to pass.

Fragments of memory came back: his visit to the station, Ludde's descent down the pipe, the explosions. There were only fragments—horrendous images that implied the impossible—

But no. He scooted to the window. A gaping wound had opened in the ice. A circular chunk of the sheet had been blown off the side, reduced to a pile of rubble that trickled downhill to the sea. Freshly shorn cliffs towered above it all. The scar that marked the new boundary between the Greenland ice and the rest of the world. On either side of the open pit, the ice sheet descended gradually towards the coast, as it had for centuries. Glaciers calve all the time, but Niels had never heard of something like this. It would only take a few summers for the ice rubble to melt entirely. And then the scattered remnants of steel walls and pipes among the barren rock would be the only sign that one of nature's grandest creations had stood there, and that a handful of humans tried to protect it.

Niels needed to talk to somebody. There was no response from his comms. His mental interface was out. Must have been the hit to the head.

Wait. His comms were out. There were people looking for him. People he couldn't hear.

He ripped the headset off the dashboard, turned a few knobs to find the Zackenberg frequency, and spoke.

"Niels!" Päivi blurted. He turned down the volume.

"This is Niels. I'm okay," he said.

He could feel their tears from across the continent. He couldn't pick out individual words in the mess, but he didn't need to.

"I'm okay," he repeated, twice. Everyone took a few minutes to calm down, then Niels explained what happened. "The station is gone. The ice is gone. It collapsed all the way to the ground, into nothing. It is just a pile of dust."

He took a photograph with the plane's camera and sent it to them. Marina gasped. It was the kind of surprise not even decades of study could prepare you for.

"You were down there?" Päivi said.

"I think, yes. I don't remember it all."

"I can't believe you got away," Rasmus said.

"Me too," Niels said. His brain had yet to accept that he'd peered over life's edge and locked eyes with oblivion. The thoughts behind his eyes seemed unreal, a part of both the material world and the one beyond. "Ludde saved my life," he said. "She got me to the plane while I was hurt."

"Hurt how?" Päivi said.

"I think I have a concussion and that my leg is broken."

"Well do not plug into the plane. Yes?" she returned. "Niels? You know this? Let Ludde drive back and you rest. Then I will fly you to Reykjavík right away."

There was more idle chatter. Niels turned down the volume and zoned out. To the southeast the sky had turned mauve, bringing enough light to reveal the boundaries between the open water and the ice-carved hills of a snowy inland bay. The stars were hiding. It'd been months since the sky had been that bright at Zackenberg.

A hundred kilometers away, by the coast, a handful of fishing towns were asleep. The destruction may not have woken them up. They'd find out soon. Niels wondered who they would blame.

"Did you talk to Igloolik, Marina?" Niels said. "Do they know who is out there?"

"They've seen no one."

Niels asked Ludde to circle the area with the plane. The water, sky, and land were empty. The radar was silent. No cruisers, artillery, or circling fighter jets. No unidentifiable flying objects. Nothing but the natural formations of the Earth, and the unblemished gradient of a slow northern sunrise.

Niels felt cheated. He craved retribution, to meet the aggressor eye-to-eye and demand an explanation. A chase, if it came to it. In his twenty-year-old plane, without guns or tags. Armed with nothing but his self-appointed position from the moral high ground. Maybe that was worth something. Why else would they have listened to his hails for peace? What does the boy with the magnifying glass feel when an ant talks back?

Perhaps this was their way of offering a second chance. If only they'd suggested what he do with it. Was he supposed to give up on Greenland? Apparently, the ice was expendable. Niels could already see next week's articles describing the destruction of the ice, and the ensuing hot potato of blame that would circulate in press conferences until another insane headline appeared and everyone would forget. Somewhere, far away from Zackenberg, people were forging the future without him. He'd only been caught in the crossfire.

Ludde beeped, highlighting the remaining amount of their carefully portioned fuel reserves. They couldn't afford a chase, anyways. Not without asking for a ride back home.

Niels sighed and said to the drone, "Let's go."

When he pulled into the hangar everyone was waiting for him. Niels carefully lowered off the seat so he could greet them at their level. He planned on not making a scene, but on his way down he saw their faces out the window. By the time the door lifted he couldn't make a sound except for a few sobs.

Rasmus grabbed Niels's shoulders with both hands, wanting desperately to give his friend a hug, but he was unsure what parts of him were hurt. Päivi asked Niels questions like what his full name was, how old he was, where he was born, and Niels answered them all until he became too embarrassed and asked to stop. He was okay. A little banged up, and he'd had his bell rung, but he'd make it. Marina entered with a pot of mint tea and some mugs, and they sat in silence. They'd lost two whole stations. There were decisions to be made, options to weigh, corrections to put into motion, and they all had ideas—but now was not the time. The specter of death lurked around the corner, watching. He would leave shortly, but not before they understood just how close Niels came to going with him. Päivi broke the tension to suggest they hurry to the hospital. Niels and his throbbing leg welcomed the idea.

Niels and Päivi didn't speak during take-off. Päivi thought she should talk to him, in case he was meditating alone on heavy thoughts like the fragility of life, or something. But she couldn't find the courage. She felt ill-equipped, and like it wasn't her place. When they got out over the Greenland Sea and settled into a comfortable cruise, Niels spoke up.

"Do you ever feel like we are all on a sinking ship?" he said, carefully, reluctantly, "And me, and you, and the others, are helping, throwing water over the sides, but then there's some *skidespræller* in the other corner shooting new holes into the bottom of the boat, and no one's stopping him."

Päivi turned around. "It is scary to face someone with a gun."

Niels looked out the window. The sky was completely clouded. Colorless, and shapeless.

"Are you certain we are on a sinking ship?" she asked.

"It seems obvious," Niels replied, with a worse tone than he'd intended.

Päivi slipped into thought. "I see it like we live on a mountain range, surrounded by the ocean, and the water keeps rising and rising, turning the peaks into islands."

Niels looked at his advisor now. "Is that so different?"

"The water will stop at some point. My whole career is set on that belief," Päivi said. "And when it does, maybe it won't be so bad. It depends who is stuck on your island with you."

There was silence in the cabin. Prof. Hallamaa continued, "Do you disagree, Niels? Are we doomed?"

"I'm not sure," he said. "But I suppose it is better to hold the bucket than the gun."

Eric Rust Backos

Building and Loan

"WE'RE OPEN AGAIN now that the water main break is fixed." Ian Lawson, the credit union manager, could see that the city services crew in their tattered, bilious safety-green raingear had put the last of the hot patch into the hole in the old brick street. They were taking up the last of the battered orange barrels as he spoke. The cash-strapped city's fix-on-failure policy was yet another failure in need of fixing.

Inside, a carpet cleaner had just finished the week's work, a delivery van arrived with a fresh doormat for the lobby, and the tellers busied about with the day's preparations.

Managing a credit union in a backwater is never dull. He looked out the ugly 1960s-vintage front window. Some forgotten remodeler had replaced a flat shopfront with a four-sided bay window of irregular polygons. It had water problems evidenced by a corroding lintel and efflorescence down either side of the frame. Fortunately, the rest of the building was old enough to be solid.

Could the weather be any worse this year? December is supposed to be snowy, isn't it? Cold rain and gusts hard enough to make the drops go sideways seemed more tropical than the week before New Year's Day should be.

The manager sat down at his desk and answered the phone. "You got rained out? Sure, I can squeeze you in ... say, two?" A pause. "No, come on in. We don't require neckties."

The carpet cleaner dragged his machine out the door into the relentless rain.

A local credit union was, in theory, an anachronism. This one, in fact, was quite popular with the myriad small businesses that still used cash in this ragged remnant of a factory town and its port on Lake Erie. Between the college, the public boat landing, and the beach, there was still a need for small businesses and a small almost-bank. Ian and the tellers stayed busy with walk-ins despite no announcement that normalcy had returned to the block.

56

He looked out the window just as an old, green Dodge dump truck pulled into the parking lot. Was the aqua tint of the thick window glass deliberate or an accident of age?

As Rikki Rush opened the driver's door, the manager recognized the Herbert Rush Construction logo and realized his two o'clock had arrived. Hans Rietveld exited the passenger side. Both jumped down to clear the extra six inches or so between the doorsill and the ground. They simultaneously pulled sweatshirt hoods over their ballcaps, zipped insulated canvas vests, and trotted with predatory grace toward the building. They were visibly wet on their windward sides by the time they opened the door of the tiny lobby.

The little brass bell over the door jingled. As he stepped through the door, Rikki patted the old brass plaque that announced,

EDWARDTOWN BUILDING & LOAN
AN EMERALD TRUST COMPANY
1922
A. W. RUSH ARCHITECT

Hans' vest was dark brown and was emblazoned with RIETVELD'S MACHINE SHOP AND GENERAL REPAIRS in orange, white, and blue script. The hoodie underneath proclaimed LAKELAND REPUBLIC. Rikki's vest had been tan once. It was off-white now and had no logo. An equally worn hoodie that once may have been dark gray bore a Holder College seal. Both wore red-and-gold caps advertising Edwardtown High School's rugby team. *Go Lions!*

Their business plan was practical. The manager knew perfectly well who sat before him since both of their grandfathers' companies were long-time customers at the tattered little credit union, and both grandfathers had asked Ian to give the boys an audience. That, and he was an EHS booster who made a professional duty of going to all the games — not that he minded it a bit ... though he still found the replacement of football and its elitism with egalitarian rugby disconcerting.

On the other hand, Hans at wing and Rikki at flanker regularly added new and complex plays to an already fast-moving game. The manager wondered if their object was to give everyone on the team a chance to score.

Ever social, Hans did the talking. A third-generation member of the South African expat community that arrived as Apartheid rule became steadily less tolerable, he looked Afrikaner with fair skin, black hair and ice-blue eyes, although his accent was native Western Reserve.

Ever morose, and a typical scion of the Connecticut families who settled Ohio after the Revolutionary War — brownish hair, green eyes, and a skin tone that suggested ancestry not entirely English — Rikki had done the writing and drawn the charts. He provided the facts and numbers in support of Hans' sales pitch with the dour demeanor of a shopkeeper getting down to the brass tacks embedded in the counter.

"Let me get this straight ... You want to buy the Bide-A-Wee Motor Court and Kate's Café, and instead of knocking down those hideous heaps of Googie style ... you want to fix them up and run them?" Ian was exactly the right age to remember when Mid-Century architecture was out enough to be embarrassingly tasteless.

"Right. The buildings are in a good spot for traffic, and between advertising to budget-minded business travelers and selling premium packages to hipsters who like the vibe, they should be profitable after minimum improvements."

Rikki proffered a chart showing traffic flows and another with an outline of barebones motel upgrades and more serious kitchen improvements.

"Who drew the kitchen?"

Hans pointed at Rikki. "He used his great-great-uncle's drafting tools."

"Asher Rush designed this building," Rikki volunteered. "His son designed the motel."

"With the same tools," Hans added.

The manager considered the high school boys asking for a loan. Considering their respective families' resources and the quality of the business plan, they could begin work on the project even before they graduated in eighteen months.

Some of the technical details surprised Ian. "Salt pool's a nice touch ... but why are you reopening the well, adding a wind turbine, and building your own wastewater treatment? Batch plants like that are usually for trailer parks and backroads without city sewers."

"The well is in use. That's what fills the pool. The well pipes to the diner, too, but city water and sewer were added in 1970. The turbine runs—will run, rather— the electric pumps and the batch plant—did you know that the sewer system has never been upgraded? With the state replacing paved roads with macadam and power companies rationing electricity, planning ahead makes good business sense."

"How are you going to run the lights and air conditioning?"

"The turbine is a stopgap. A natural-gas generator is a possible second stop-gap. Phase two replaces the solid windows with operating ones and adds ceiling fans."

Ian didn't notice that the proposed ceiling fans were belt-driven in the sketch. Rikki produced several more charts showing the potential for profit.

"Okay. What's the long-term goal here?" There was something amiss in all the scrambling to revive some old buildings. Too much emphasis on water and gas on the property. And the whole mess had been on the market far too long. Why a big developer hadn't shown up yet was beyond him. Like most people, the manager had a sense that there was something wrong with the economy, yet still expected the rebound that remained elusively around the corner.

"We'd like to own a string of motels for the budget-conscious traveler. Clean, no frills, low overhead. We'd like pools and diners to be our signature amenities. Reviving buildings on major highways ..."

"Not that, I mean, what's the big dream that has you dreaming big?"

Hans was a little hurt by the interruption. He'd practiced his pitch. A. LOT. Rikki glanced at him, then pulled another folder from the borrowed oxblood leather portfolio in his lap.

Their complicated plays and fast footwork on the rugby field crossed the manager's mind. The boys had practiced their delivery, but he wanted to see the off-topic origin of their plan.

"Most kids don't ask for a motel for a graduation present. How big is your dream?"

Hans spoke clearly and firmly, as if delivering very bad news to a good customer. The manager recognized the source of Hans' style and smiled to himself.

"We think," Hans began, "climate change is going to disrupt the weather patterns and affect the economy enough that a budget-price but respectable hotel chain along major highways will be profitable. If the Midwest and Northeast warm a bit as the Southwest dries out, most of the year will be cool, not cold, and rainy. We won't need the AC, but we will still need heat. If the Great Lakes region ends up dried out because the Arctic ice cap melts and shifts the weather patterns north, we'll have a string of ready-made caravansaries for the five-state region."

Caravans? A thousand and one images from a lifetime of American pop culture blew through Ian's mind like sand grains in a desert breeze.

"Well ..." The manager paused and considered what the Rietvelds were known to do to pickup trucks. "Well, that's a stretch ... so ... why?"

Rikki finally spoke. "A writer we like challenged us."

"To run a motel?"

"Not exactly. He said to imagine our lives in 'a future of gradual economic contraction, social turmoil, and technological regression.' Not hard, right?"

The manager boggled at the idea that the current economy was anything but temporary, but he remained poker-faced.

Rikki didn't notice. He continued, "The follow-up challenge, 'Your goal is to envision ways in which you and those you care about can lead creative, humane, and meaningful lives in such a time,' is a ..."

"Tall order." The manager de-boggled his mind, considered the boys and concluded that they were quite serious.

Hans and Rikki traded looks.

Hans said, "The trick to doing those things is avoiding the urge to do nothing."

Glancing at the wall clock strategically placed behind his customers caused Ian to realize decision time had arrived. Rain was still visible through the peculiar angles of the front window, though it was a normal cold drizzle now.

"All the numbers pencil, and I like your ideas. You can tell your grandfathers I'm willing to finance your motel project."

Too young to sign for a loan, the boys shook hands, said the usual things, and went out the door.

As they were walking out, a worn, white International pickup with faded lettering on the doors reading Cobble Knoll Farms in green on a large red apple pulled up and parked a few spaces from Rikki's Dodge.

The manager looked up from his desk just in time to see the driver, a slight, red-haired girl wearing the same look as the boys, bounce out of the cab and kiss Rikki. A taller, better-dressed woman exited the passenger side. Ah. Catherine Morton and her daughter … He glanced at the forms in front of him. Bellavee, yes, that's it.

"My three o'clock is here early," he said to the head teller.

"Nice to see Hippie Hollow is back in business."

"Let's see if we can keep it that way."

Ian looked at Rikki as he climbed into the battered truck. Maybe Cobble Knoll won't be the only comeback, he thought.

Clint Spivey

The Optometrist's Apprentice

THE TREMORS WERE BACK, right alongside a tightening chest and racing heart. Art's hand shook with enough violence that he feared flinging the eyeglass-arm across his cluttered little workshop. He counted deep breaths, hoping to quiet the rising panic attack and still his shaking hands by willpower alone.

The shakes continued, as did Art's anxiety.

The frames were secure in a tiny relic vise from before the riot-times. He'd attached the left arm successfully, inserting the tiny screw before turning it tight. It was when he'd begun work on the glasses' right arm that the attack began.

The tiny screw, lying on its side, rested atop the hole joining arm and frame. With another deep breath, Art stilled the shakes and inserted the eyeglass-arm with his left hand, lining up the holes so he might insert the screw. Holding the small screwdriver with his right hand, he aimed for the screw. The spasms returned.

He pulled back in terror of sending the screw tumbling to the warped wooden floor, where it would most certainly be lost. The screw, a miracle of pre-riot precision, was almost as valuable as the scavenged lenses he'd earlier in-serted into the eyeglass frames. Losing the screw meant he'd need to cannibalize another set of glasses, and attempt the delicate procedure all over again.

Art set down the screwdriver and slid his hand into the pocket of his faded jeans, worrying the empty plastic medicine bottle like a talisman. It had been left unfilled for decades, but just touching it occasionally quieted his anxieties.

Instead of peace, touching it only summoned the voice of his long dead father. "Worthless Millennial. Real men don't need pills to deal with life." Decades in the grave and the man still haunted Art with the same insults. "You'll drop that screw then the town will drop you. Good luck being woke beyond the walls."

Doorway chimes tinkled in the lobby beyond the curtain separating it from his workshop. The banker's bell at the counter soon rang to life.

"You alive back there, Arturo?"

It was Dolores, there to retrieve her glasses. He'd thought he'd have time to finish it before she returned. But he'd been busy. Too many other patients. Other orders. He simply couldn't keep up.

"Be right with you," he said, feigning nonchalance. He gritted his teeth, and inserted the arm into the frame. He tried matching the shakes, rolling with them as he attempted to master his hands. Holding his breath, trying to ignore his father's mockery, he touched the screwdriver's magnetic tip to the tiny screw.

He almost cried. The screw dropped into the hole connecting the arm to the frame. Before he could lose it again he tightened it into place, and breathed. He removed them from the tiny vise and rose, cleaning the lenses with a piece of chamois, more pre-riot salvage.

Setting the glasses down, he removed the plastic bottle from his pocket, uncapped it, and mimed swallowing one of his meds. The panic, a thing gnawing for purchase in his mind, receded.

"What do you think?" he asked after joining Dolores in the lobby and handing over the glasses.

Her gray hair was tied in a ponytail. She was tanned and muscled from her many days escorting coal-caravans on horseback. Dolores was younger than Art's seven decades by at least two. But even his age couldn't diminish the fluttering warmth that rose whenever they met. She removed her old glasses, scratched and black with coal dust, and donned the new ones.

Art grinned. The slim, black frames fit her face perfectly.

"Perfect," she said, as if lifting the word from his thoughts. "Finally got me some city glasses. I'll be by later with your pay."

He tried to protest that he was happy to help, but she wouldn't hear of it.

"I don't need any charity and neither do you. Once we get things unloaded and I've had a bite and a bath, I'll be back."

"Where's the caravan?" Art asked, looking past her. The dusty street beyond his storefront was empty but for her wagon.

"Stopped out at Vicky's place. She had juice for us all but they're probably half drunk on her cider by now. As much as I like lounging in the orchards I needed to get back."

She thanked him once more, with a hearty handshake and a shoulder grab that sent Art's heart thudding, and made for the door.

"Oh." She paused beneath the tinkling chimes above the entrance. "The caravan's got a surprise for you. I think you'll like it. Some big changes are being whispered about." She winked, and departed.

Surprise? Had she finally noticed him? As the oldest in Werther he often felt the loneliest. But lonely didn't mean without dreams. And Dolores was often in his.

He followed her outside into the dusty August afternoon.

"Still waiting on winning the lottery, eh? Your big break?" His father again. "You're all the same. Can't focus on your job 'cause you're always waiting to make it big. Just like you almost messed up those glasses. Back in my day ..."

Whatever the town of Werther had been before the riot-times, it was much smaller after. During those frightening years its people had learned to live close in protection. And while each passing year of peace further expanded their orchards and fields beyond the town's walls, the population of around 200 still lived within the several city blocks of the old town.

Unlike most residents, Art lived alone. What was once a front lawn now boasted fruit and nut trees. He walked past them to the root-cracked sidewalk. The old residential neighborhood was now Werther's tree-lined main street. Dolores' wagon was piled with goods from her most recent trip. Werther's proximity to Coalsem provided the town with important trade. She was at the front seeing to her horses.

"Your bags packed?" a harsh voice asked from rear of the wagon. A handcuffed man, covered in dust from the journey and coaldust from the wagon, slid over to face Art.

"Petey?" Art asked. "The hell you doing back here?"

He offered a wicked smile, revealing rotting teeth.

"They need bodies at Coalsem. Kidnapped me right off the street. It's slavery, I tell you."

Art frowned. Peter Lawson had once lived in Werther, until he'd been caught peeking into one too many windows at night and the town had had enough of him. He'd been sent to Coalsem to work off his sentence. Last Art had heard he'd been living in Ferris Creek, but now it seemed he was headed right back to the mines.

"So, in other words, they caught you creeping around people's houses again?"

"Wouldn't be worrying about me if I were you. They need hands bad up at the mines. Even ones as old as yours."

"What are you talking about?" Art knew not to pay the old troublemaker much mind, yet his hand wandered to the bottle in his pocket for comfort.

"They think Petey don't listen. That I can't hear their plans. But big plans they got." He smiled again, making a show of looking around before leaning close and lowering his voice. "Did you like your replacement?"

"What replacement?" Art asked.

"Oops. Did I ruin the surprise. Oh well." He patted the coal-black wagon bed beside him. "I'll keep a spot warm for you at Coalsem."

"Lawson!" Dolores called from up near the horses. "Mouth shut and eyes front!" She mounted the board atop the wagon and, reins in hand, got the horses moving. Petey waved, his smile bigger than ever.

Art stood for several minutes in the baking sun before returning inside. The old living room had been refurbished into an examination center and repair shop for eye-wear. With a salvaged phoropter and eye chart, Art attempted to match surplus glasses to patients.

People had learned to live without a lot of things after the riot-times. Poor vision wasn't one of them. Fortunately, pre-riot manufacturing had left piles of old eyewear lying about for salvage. He occasionally diagnosed situations requiring specific meds or surgeries, but those patients required care outside of what Werther could provide. Other than treating a few occasional eye injuries, Art mostly dealt with vision correction.

Thus, as the riot-times settled to something resembling order, Art found himself with a useful skill in the nearest town to the vital Coalsem mines where the residents tolerated him despite his age.

At least, that's what he'd thought. Had they finally tired of him? Art's heart began to race.

He pulled the bottle from his pocket. Uncapped it, and mimed taking a pill. The little mindfulness performance had been something he devised after prescriptions had long since vanished. He slowed his breaths to try and master the rising anxiety.

"Looks like you'll finally get the taste of some real work," his father whispered. "Maybe the mines'll make a *real* man out of you ... but I doubt it."

With his father's words lingering, he headed out back to speak with the Duchess.

The late afternoon sun had dropped beneath the sprawling walnut tree shading much of the backyard. The tiny terrier napped beside the back door.

"Another hot one, eh?" he said. The Duchess looked at him without rising through her one good eye, the other clouded over and useless.

He'd found more luck than he felt due in Werther. That the town tolerated one so old as him was testament to the kind of place it was. He couldn't help much in the orchards or fields. He tried making up for this by remaining useful in his little optometry clinic. He thought he'd been doing a good job of it, too. Nearly half the town had utilized his services at some point. Why would they want him gone?

"You wouldn't want me gone, would you?" he asked.

The Duchess went back to sleep.

Peter was a liar and a criminal. What did Art have to worry about? Leaving Her Highness to her napping, he returned to his shop to finish up the day's work.

The stranger waiting inside greeted him with a smile.

☉

Art knew just about everyone in Werther, but he was certain he'd never met the young man standing before him.

"You must be Art." He extended a hand. "I'm Lenny. Looking forward to working together."

Art shook his hand. "Working?" he said uncertainly. "I don't understand."

The man knelt to look inside a display case full of glasses. "Didn't Dolly come to see you?"

"Dolly?" Art's confusion deepened. The man looked to be mid- to late thirties with bright red hair that hadn't even begun to thin. Sporting a neatly trimmed beard, he was handsome and lean. Art reached for his empty bottle.

The man stood. "Sorry. That's what I called Dolores on the trip over from Ferris Creek. She's quite the talker."

A lump swelled in Art's throat. "Um. Yeah. She sure is." He tried for a smile. "But I'm not sure--"

The chimes above his door came to life.

"Ah," Dolores said entering with a grin. "You two found each other."

Art's smile curled to a grimace.

"Lenny's your new apprentice," Dolores said, clapping the man on the shoulder.

Petey's words came back to him. The surprise the caravan had brought. The waiting mines.

"An apprentice," Art said weakly.

"Yep," Dolores said. "To help take some of the work off your hands. Rode the caravan back with us."

Art just stared while Lenny and Dolores chatted on about life in Werther.

"You thought they'd keep you forever?" his father whispered. Art could still see the man lit with the vitriolic glow of 24-hour cable TV news. "You're used up. And you're the only one who doesn't know it yet."

"Art?" Dolores said, interrupting his thoughts.

"Sorry, yes?"

"C'mon. We've got something to show you."

"Well I'll be damned," Art said, as Lenny set the heavy piece of equipment on the table with care. They'd wisely wrapped it in cloth, ignorant of its purpose, but understanding its worth. "Where'd you find it?"

Dolores frowned. "First tell us what the hell is it."

Art endured popping knees to kneel for a better look. "A lensometer," he said, peering into the eyepiece.

"I knew it!" Lenny snapped his fingers. "Never used one, but I've heard of them. But how the hell's it work?"

Art stood up from his examination of the device. "You're not an optician?"

Lenny shook his head. "Nope. Started my associate's. Well, back before the riot-times. But I *did* work in a vision center. Back then they were hiring any warm body."

"Enough with the suspense!" Dolores said. "What does the damned thing even do?"

Art smiled. The joy at being useful, at being *needed*, chased away thoughts of his father.

"It lets you determine a prescription just from a lens," Art said. "I'll be able to find almost perfect glasses with this."

"Shouldn't draw too much power," Dolores said, examining the device's black power cord. "Less than *that* I imagine," she said motioning to the phoropter in the converted living room. "But let someone know if your solar setup needs tweaking. Wait." She dropped the cord she'd been holding. "How were you checking prescriptions before?" Dolores asked.

"Tell her," came his father. "Tell her how you were faking it all this time."

Occasionally lenses were found still within their paper sleeves with printed prescription information, but these were rare. What had mostly survived the looted big-box stores and clinics were glasses already assembled. Art explained how he'd sorted this salvage as best he could. Then simply resorted to trial-and-error to match best what he had to his patient's needs following an exam.

"So this thing's gonna put you out of a job," Dolores joked, Lenny joining in her laughter.

Art continued his inspection of the lensometer. How quick his comfort evaporated. His anxiety flooded back alongside a mirthless chuckle from his long dead father.

As if reading his thoughts, and in a hurry to rid the town of such a relic as Art, Lenny asked for a demonstration of the lensometer.

"Tomorrow," Art said.

Art ate alone that night. Even with the fuel they got from Coalsem, cooking was mostly done communally. Heating a few large stoves in the dining hall was far more efficient than portioning out fuel to every household for meals. Art had brought that night's stew home. A few looks and whispers from the townspeople at dinner only confirmed his suspicions and convinced him to get his meal to-go.

His chest tightened, an uncomfortable feeling while young that carried sheer terror at his current age. He would die at Coalsem. Of that he was certain. Even worse was the seeming comfort of the citizens of Werther with this fact. If they were to exile him to the mines, then his death obviously troubled them little.

"And why should it? A soft man from a soft time. Only thing that kept you alive was pure, dumb, blind luck. And that luck is gone. Hard times now. And hard men. No place for soft woke ones."

Art stared at his stew. Candlelight gleamed from the spoonful of broth. He generally saved his solar to operate the clinic. The candlelight was usually comforting.

This night, the flickering shadows felt foreboding.

His hand started to shake. He felt the tears beginning to well. Art hated his father. And knew the words of a long-dead fool shouldn't be able to hurt him. But they did. Across the years and from beneath the ground. From some forgotten corpse in whatever hole the man had been laid in, unmourned and unloved, his miserable father still held Art within his bullying grasp.

The next few days saw Art grateful for Lenny's help and in positive dread of how little he could keep up with his new apprentice. Each day followed a pattern of introductions of his handsome partner to beaming patients while Art struggled to demonstrate his remaining utility.

"You line up these lines first," Art said, adjusting the knob on the lensometer's side until the lines were in focus. "That's your sphere." Art marked the value. "Turn this knob until *these* lines, the fat ones, are in focus. That's your cylinder."

"I kept trying to get both sets in focus at once," Lenny said. "Makes so much more sense now. Thanks."

Art removed the eyeglasses from the lensometer tray while nodding.

It would have been easier if Lenny wasn't so damned charming and likable. Despite his growing dread, Art found himself enjoying the lightened workload while often joining in the laughter at Lenny's jokes with a patient. Even their past, pre-riot lives had been similar. Art had worked in a big-box-store vision center same as Lenny. One of the best-paying gigs he could get after the crushing student debt was as an optometrist. The two recounted almost identical tales of watching society crumble from within the vision center's windows.

"We'd get busy," Lenny had recounted. "But people were generally relaxed or calm. But everyone outside the clinic. Always arguing or coming to blows for overpriced food. Berating staff. The vision center always felt ... I dunno ..."

"Safe?" Art asked. It was a feeling he remembered well. A feeling he'd grown accustomed to while living within Werther's walls.

Lenny looked across the old living-room-turned-exam-area and ran a hand through his thick, red hair. "Safe. Yeah."

His thoughts wandered once more to Coalsem. To the degenerate Petey and his words. The more time he spent with Lenny, the more Art began questioning whether the man had been telling the truth. It had been nearly a week since Lenny had arrived. And Art still had a place in the town. Hadn't been rousted in the night and taken to the mines. Art began entertaining the comforting thought that Petey—always the liar and self-proclaimed victim—had simply been doing what he always had. Which was spreading bullshit. Art decided then to broach the subject with Lenny.

"How are things in Ferris?" he asked.

"Oh, you know," Lenny said while assembling a pair of glasses from cannibalized parts. "Same as here, I guess. More things to do with the river. Fishing and stuff."

"Any problems coming back with the caravan?" Art asked while wiping down the patient chair beneath the hanging phoropter.

"Nope. No one's tryna be a bandit anymore. That shit got old. Much easier to eat working in town. All the trouble is within the walls these days."

"Yeah," Art said with a tone as if he'd just remembered something. "Didn't you guys bring someone back with you? Bound for Coalsem because of trouble."

Lenny snorted. "Garbage-Breath Pete? Yeah. Liked to look through people's windows. Picked the wrong one and caught a beatdown from some kid's parents."

"Oh?" Again, Art tried for surprise. "Yeah, he's from here originally. Did the same thing and was sent to the mines."

Lenny held up his completed work, angling the lenses toward the light to check for scratches. "Well he must like it there, 'cause he went right back."

"What was it like with him on the wagon? He have anything to say?"

"Wasn't anyone listening to that dumbass. I was up front with Dolores the whole way. We had other things to discuss."

"What were you guys talking about?" Art instantly regretted the eagerness of the question.

Lenny put down the glasses. "We talked about a lot of things, Dolores and me. Mostly about here in Werther. And the job. You know." He looked at Art and smiled. "She told me about some old curmudgeon I'd be working with. Said his dog was the better part of the gig." He laughed before bending down to scratch The Duchess behind the ear. "Just kidding, man."

Art laughed with him, returning to his work cleaning the phoropter. A warm feeling suffused him. As much as he'd learned pre-riot about his anxiety and the paranoia it dragged with it, he often neglected how wrong it usually was. Dreaded events that never materialized. Crippling worries about some perceived insult to a person that amounted to nothing. And like so many times before, he'd let his anxiety devour him over Petey's lies.

He smiled. No stinging insults came from his father. His hand didn't wander to his empty bottle of meds. Art just continued on with his work.

⊙

The next day brought a crispness with it that whispered of the coming autumn beneath a clear blue sky streaked with high cirrus. Art breakfasted with a happiness he hadn't felt in days.

"And how we doing this morning?" he asked while scooping food into the Duchess's bowl. Art placed the bowl near the back door, propping it open for her to exit out back when she was ready. She wandered over and sniffed at the food before taking a few bites. Art had just begun the arduous process of standing up when he heard voices from outside.

"Why can't *you* tell him?" a man said quietly. Was that Lenny?

"Because I'm not the one with him all day. If I go telling him he might get spooked and the whole thing's out the window."

Art, still kneeling at the back door, nearly fell over. The other speaker was Dolores.

"I don't like this secrecy," Lenny said. "Just tell him. He's a grown man. He can handle it."

"No. He's been here too long to just blurt out, 'Oh hey, guess what, Art? Blah blah.' No. Just keep him busy till tonight."

As if this couldn't shake Art further, Dolores spoke once more.

"What the matter, Lenny?" she asked, her voice taking a playful tone that sent Art wincing. "A little intrigue too much for a Ferris boy?"

Art stood, ignoring the pain and pops of his aged knees. He didn't want to hear what came next. What casual conspiracy the two plotted while flirting. He looked around in a daze, when an old, familiar sound greeted him.

It started low, a rasping laughter that grew more mocking as it built enthusiasm. There were no words or insults. Just the gleeful mirth his father had always saved for reveling in the misfortune of others.

Of course they were to be rid of him. Why had he thought differently? He didn't even bother with his medicine bottle. If even Dolores — the woman he'd pined over for years — was ready to discard him so casually, why bother with the charade of his meds.

Dragging his feet like a shambling zombie, he made ready to open the shop.

"What kind of meeting?" Art asked later that morning.

"They didn't say," Lenny answered without looking up from his work. He'd created a neat little assembly line around the lensometer, carefully checking each pair of glasses before scribbling down the prescription on scrap paper and tucking it tight between the closed arms. Impressive rows of completed work lined the bench beside him.

Art had tried to hide his fear. The rising panic threatening to send him into shaking sobs. Almost as if pretending normalcy might stay his dismissal.

"They *did* say not to be late," Lenny said. "Dolores made me promise to tell you."

"Got a bag packed?" his father mocked. "Maybe they'll let you take your support dog to hug between shifts down the mine."

The bell jingled at the front door. The Duchess looked up from where she lazed beside the display case.

"Hi," said Lenny, hurrying to the counter while Art was still squinting to see who'd entered.

"Oh," the young woman said. "Hi."

"Hi Ruthie," Art said, joining Lenny at the counter. "What can I—we do for you?"

Art remembered when she'd first come in for glasses as a child with her parents. She'd been the last patient that winter day and the sun had already set. Once he'd checked her vision and found a suitable pair of glasses, she'd been stunned at how clear the world became. He especially remembered her joy at seeing the lights. The candles glowing in the storefront windows. The crisp stars in the clear winter air. A whole world, invisible just moments prior, had been revealed that night.

How fast the years passed. Ruthie was in her twenties now and had returned to the shop many times over the years to update her prescription.

"I'm Lenny," he said. "What can we help you with?"

She removed her glasses. "Can you tighten these?" she asked, demonstrating the loose arms by swinging them. "We don't have a small enough screwdriver at home."

"Sure thing," Lenny said, taking her glasses. "Won't take but a minute."

Her hands were stained with various colors of paint, more than usual. "Working on something new?" Art asked, nodding to her hands.

She glanced at them both before dropping them to her sides. "Oh. Um, not really. Hey, Duchess." She leaned down and scratched behind the dog's ears.

Ruthie had always been pleasant with Art, even chatty.

Now? Even *she* wouldn't look him in the eye.

"They all know," his father said. "Know you're on the way out."

"Thank you," she said after Lenny handed back her glasses. She hurried out without another word.

All that afternoon he thought of the meeting. People avoided him throughout the day, averted their gaze while passing in the street. It was the final indignity. Reduced to refuse, about to be tossed out, they didn't even bother regarding him.

Even Lenny found some excuse to cut out early.

Long shadows stretched across the exam room. High cirrus clouds were a riot of red and orange in the setting sun. Watching the beautiful scene through the window, Art knew what he had to do.

Should he tell them? Attend their little soiree and meekly accept his exile? No. He could do this one final act alone. Whatever agency a seventy-three-year-old possessed, he'd exercise it now. He'd deny them his discomfort, and depart on his own.

"First good call you've made in your comfy little life," his father wheezed. "Save the real men of this town the trouble of burying you. Feed the wolves beyond the wall. Give flesh to the true alphas."

Art realized how vacuous the words were, and not for the first time considered them nothing more than his anxiety whispering in his head. But it didn't matter. The town wanted him gone. He popped an invisible pill.

He started packing a backpack. With little plan other than to walk into the scorching, late-summer wastes, he packed light. The Duchess stirred and, sensing something awry, trotted toward him.

"Not you, Your Highness." He knelt and smiled while scratching the little terrier behind her ears. "You stay."

A sense of calm overcame him. His first major decision in years bringing comfort if not joy. Why stay with those who don't want you around?

His thoughts wandered. Back to times pre-riot. His few failed attempts at dating. A similar sensation. Ghosting some partner who only wanted to be friends. Was he acting in a similar childish manner?

No. This was different. He wouldn't let himself be sent to Coalsem. The final remnants of value dragged from his withered body for a few cartloads of coal. He shouldered his pack, grabbed his walking stick, and made for the back door.

The Duchess, showing some canine understanding, began whining.

"You don't wanna go where I'm headed. Someone here will take care of you. Maybe Ruthie will keep you."

She whined louder. Even managed a gruff little bark. Why would anyone keep the Duchess? If the town didn't have the patience for a used-up old man, how much would they have for a half-blind Yorkshire terrier?

He didn't know if it was right. To bring a dog alongside while walking off to die. But she didn't want to be left behind. And, despite how selfish the feeling, he didn't think he wanted to die alone.

"Alright," he said, pulling a long unused leash from the wall. "Let's bounce."

They snuck out the back rather than risk the main street. Even from there the bustling sounds of the dining hall could be heard. Had they invited the whole town to witness his exile? Some shared responsibility for sending him away? Spreading around his death sentence in order to dilute it? He turned to the orchards ringing the town, took a breath, and shuffled off to die.

The walls ringing Werther had fallen into disrepair since the riot-times had subsided, but he still had to search for a way through. Cactus, rosebushes, anything with a sticker had been planted along the fenceline, with blackberry brambles being the final barrier. The entire thing was wild tangle that even someone half his age would require a machete to clear. Before long, he was approaching the town's main gate.

He ducked behind a tree, pulled the Duchess close, and waited in the growing twilight. Nothing moved. There was usually a watch, two or more, who, riot-times gone or no, at least kept an eye on the literal comings and goings of town.

Tonight, it was abandoned.

He stood, tugged lightly at the Duchess's leash, and walked out of Werther forever.

The orchards were buzzing with crickets, the sound a comforting contrast to what he knew awaited him in the wastes beyond. He paused, turning once more toward the muted, candlelit glow of Werther behind.

"Art?"

He jerked toward the sound, his pack falling to the dirt in his panic.

"I . . . uh," he stammered in the dark, his hand instinctively going to his empty medicine bottle.

"What are you doing out here?" Dolores stepped from the shadows of the apple trees, a jug of cider in each hand. "Why aren't you at the dining hall? Damn, man. You're gonna be late for your own party!"

Seeing Dolores, her sharp features made gorgeous in the waning light, summoned an unfamiliar anger.

"Some party," he sneered. "I know what you all are planning."

She tilted her head. "You do? Dammit, who told?"

The brevity with which she spoke was infuriating. "Does it matter? I'm leaving. Saving you all the trouble. Your consciences will be clear." He picked up his pack, ignoring the pops in his knees as he did. "So long, Dolores."

"Wait! Art!" She hurried beside him, grunting with effort from the massive jugs. "What the hell are you talking about?"

He didn't want to look at her. Just stormed ahead with The Duchess at his heels.

"Petey told me everything. About Lenny. Coalsem. *Everything.*"

"Petey?" Shock vied with laughter in her voice. "What the hell are you doing listening to that fool? And what *about* Coalsem?"

He explained Petey's words. That he'd finally grown too old to be of any worth. That he was to be sent to the mines. His replacement with Lenny, ostensibly an apprentice, only confirmed this.

"And you believed Petey?" Dolores said. "*That* fool? Jackass broke his probation. He's the one back in the mines. Oh, Art." Her tone softened. "You really think we're sending you to Coalsem?"

He clenched his fist hard even though it hadn't been shaking. It was easy to cling to fears. Not so easy to let them go.

"I've seen the way no one can look me in the eye. The way they avert their gaze." Tears were beginning to well. "I'll save you all the trouble." He needed a pill. The tightness in his chest was crushing. He prayed to whoever was listening that he wouldn't have a panic attack in front of Dolores.

"We're opening a college." Her words were calm, measured. "Tonight was going to be a surprise to give you the news."

Art paused. "A college?"

"In case you hadn't noticed, you're not getting any younger. Makes a lot more sense to pass some of that knowledge on rather than work you until you drop. And this apprentice shit's for the birds. Might've worked well a thousand years ago when everyone was dumping corpses down the well. These days, makes a lot more sense to just teach a room full of students."

"A college," Art repeated, his anger lost in his confusion.

"The old campus at Dixon. All the towns have been working on this for a while. But it needed to be kept quiet until we were sure we could pull it off. No town was going to part with their lone dentist or doctor unless it was a sure thing that a suitable replacement could step in to fill the gap."

She set down the jugs of cider and took his hand in hers. "If you thought we'd send you to the mines, that we didn't appreciate you ... I'm sorry. Sorry we never let you know how much we did. That we didn't take you for granted."

"But you're sending me away? Forcing me to leave?"

"Well, we figured you might like standing around all day speaking with interested youngsters. Having your meals and housing taken care of in exchange for knowledge. While alongside a whole lot of other teachers your age. But" — she shrugged — "if you feel like working in Werther until you drop dead, who am I to stop you?"

Teaching? He'd never done it. But he definitely knew a few things about optometry. And it did sound like a nice change of pace.

Dolores went on to explain how the towns were all contributing. Doctors and dentists. Farmers and carpenters. Plumbers and barbers. Anyone with knowledge who might be getting a little long in the tooth. All alongside young people who'd tend gardens and cook meals as their tuition.

"Kind of a retirement ... at least that's what we all thought." Dolores toed the jugs of cider with her boot. "Tonight was a sort of surprise party."

Art closed his eyes. If he hadn't bumped into Dolores ...

"I thought you guys were through with me," he said.

"Never." She smiled. "Now," she said, bending down and lifting the cider.

"We're gonna be late."

They walked back to the dining hall, Art feeling happier than he had in weeks. The Duchess seemed to sense this and trotted along with more energy than Art had seen in a long time.

"Wait," Dolores said as they approached the hall. "Try and act surprised."

Art didn't have to fake it.

"Look who I found," Dolores said as the room erupted and hoots in cheers.

The room was packed. Nearly the entire town was waiting inside in front of the largest feast Art had seen since before the riot-times. Food and desserts crowded the long tables. Bottles of wine, cider, and even whiskey were in abundance. Art was seated at the head table.

Little time was wasted on speeches before people dug in. Only the pre-riot world would let such food cool under the breath of long-winded toastmasters. Instead, everything Dolores had told him of the college was presented to the entire assemblage by town leaders as people ate, drank, and listened. It wasn't until everyone had at least finished a plate that the festivities turned to Art.

A line of his patients, young and old, waited to congratulate him, showering him with praise.

"Keep a seat open for me," Lenny said, shaking Art's hand with both of his. "Once you graduate some students to take over here, it's my turn in the class. Teach a man to fish and all that."

Art beamed. "It's a deal."

Ruthie in particular wowed the entire room when she unveiled a painting she'd made just for him.

"It's beautiful," Art said with awe.

She'd masterfully captured Werther's main street at night. Familiar winter constellations lit the sky while candles glowed from each storefront window. Yet they were blurred. Fuzzy as if seen through a haze. And in the center, held by two hands, were a pair of glasses, everything within them crisp and clear and bursting with detail.

"Maybe you can hang it in your new office," Ruthie said.

Art tilted his head. "Will I have an office?"

Dolores set down her glass of whiskey. "Dunno. We'll have to ask when we arrive."

"We?" Art asked.

"Yep. I'm taking you. It's near a week to Dixon. We'll leave whenever you're packed."

He waited for his father. Reached for his medicine bottle in anticipation of some hissed harangue to darken his mood. But it never came. The man who'd bragged of never having gone to college, now had a son who'd soon be teaching at one.

Smiling, he thanked Ruthie for the painting, and sipped his cider. The Duchess, her tongue lolling as she watched for the next table-scrap dropped her way, looked happy enough for them both.

A week alone with Dolores. Art could think of worse ways to start a new job.

C. M. Barnes

BlackRabbit

"Hazel? Hazel, you there? Asia just crashed. Or perhaps you didn't notice?"

The voice came down out of a constellation of speakers built into the ceiling of Elias's study. It was Fiver calling in from his own urban fortress up in the Bay—or whatever was left of the Bay.

"Morning, Fiver," Elias replied to the ceiling.

"It's 1 A.M."

"Technically, still morning, my friend."

"Funny." Fiver's voice was a nasally whine. "And what about Asia?"

"Not too worried about it. Some scraggly pack of Luddies attacked a cable in Mongolia or something. The ground bots will fix it, and we'll be up and running before European markets open."

"Wish I shared your sense of serenity."

"I don't. Your job is to worry, Fiver, and you do it well."

Silence gathered in the speakers above. It probably wasn't a good idea to mess with Fiver, not this early in the morning. He would have just had his special, heart-pounding blend of Ethiopian coffee droned in. It made him even more jumpy than usual.

"You don't want me to call Bigwig?" Fiver said. "You don't think security should at least *look* at this?"

Elias pressed a switch on the arm of his chair and began to spin himself around. He'd been in the chair since 7 P.M. As head of the company, he felt it was his duty to pull his share of nightshifts. "Fine," he said. "Call Bigwig. But don't be too alarmist about it. He's been up and ready to whoop virtual ass since midnight his time. I don't want him crashing the whole system just to murder some drifter code the digi-bots will take care of anyway."

Silence built overhead. Elias waited for it to break, still spinning.

"Is this the right time to tell you I've got a bad feeling?" Fiver said.

Elias stopped spinning. "How bad?"

"Pretty bad."

"Australia bad?"

"Maybe worse."

"Did you just drink that defibrillator joe you like? That shit is fusion in a cup—"

"I've got a *bad* feeling, Hazel."

"Let me take another look."

Elias pressed the arm switch forward and waved his screen up. Worldwide, the system looked basically fine—Asia notwithstanding. A few other scattered dead zones in Africa and South America. Nothing outside the norm. One of them resolved itself over Johannesburg as he watched.

"Not seeing much, but your feeling is duly noted. I'll man the desk for another hour."

"Not like you sleep."

"Guilty. But, speaking of, lay off that go-juice, will you? Can't afford to lose you to another *palpitation*—"

Elias's screen turned bright red. Then Europe went dark.

"Ah, shit," Fiver said. "Europe's down."

"Saw that."

"Can I get Bigwig now?"

"Yeah ... and Blueberry too. Might need the Whiz Kid."

"What about Holly?"

Elias stared at the handsome, mahogany-paneled ceiling above him. Such wood did not come cheap, especially in a world increasingly devoid of trees. He did some quick cost calculating. "Hold off on Holly," he said. "Don't think we need the cavalry yet."

"European markets open in half an hour."

"Aware of that. Any intel on extra Luddie activity in Europe recently? I think there's some wicked bat plague ripping through the Balkans. Always tends to rile them up."

"Negative. Do we think this is external?"

"Has to be. Nothing on the inside could crash a continent without triggering a shitload of digi-bots first."

"You sure?"

"Who designed this thing, Baby?"

"I've got Bigwig."

"Patch the man through."

Elias frowned at his screen while he waited for his head of security to report. Europe was still dark. So was Asia, and now there was some weird, spotty activity going over North Africa. His gaze shifted inadvertently to the permanent black hole that had been Australia. Technically, it was still Australia, but, after the big burn of '37, it might as well have been the moon. There were probably still some Luddies living down there. Maybe they were out in—what did they used to call it?—*the bush*. They definitely weren't sunbathing on those charred-up coasts.

"What up, Hazel?" Bigwig growled from the ceiling. "Got us some early-morning silliness to deal with?"

"Late-night silliness to be precise," Fiver said.

"Not here in the Citizen's Republic of Greater New York. It's after four. Sun will be up in an hour, provided we can see it through the smoke."

"What do you got for me, Big Guy?" Elias said. "Any OWSLA code you can run to clear Europe's pipes? We got markets opening in less than half an hour. Money's got to move."

"Looking into it, Chief."

"I got Blueberry too," Fiver said.

"Morning, Whiz Kid. Stand by to work your magic."

"Roger that," Blueberry's charming southern accent descended into the room. Elias congratulated himself once again for bringing Blueberry onto the team. Talent wasn't easy to acquire these days, especially when it was situated in the New Confederacy, but Blueberry was worth every digi-dollar.

"All right. Getting something," Bigwig said. "Looks like … Nope. Can't be right."

"What?" Elias said.

"Yeah, *what?*" Fiver echoed. "Is it bad? I bet it's bad."

"No," Bigwig said. "Maybe. I don't know. It's definitely *weird*."

"Weird how?" Elias said.

"It's the system. All the usual elements are online and running fine, even in Asia. It's just … there's an extra one."

"An *extra* one?" Elias said. What the fuck was that? And, more importantly, how could whatever it was get un-fucked in the next—he checked New Greenwich Mean on his desk panel—25 minutes? "Need more info. Fiver, Blueberry, run your own diagnostics and feel free to chime in. All-hands-on-deck time."

"Meaning I should get Holly?"

"No, Fiver. Let's just try to figure this thing out for a second."

Elias launched his diagnostic program. Bigwig was right. Everything was running fine—aside from the fact that not much was actually *running*, not in Asia, not in Europe, and now not in Africa. Money had come to a stop everywhere in the Eastern Hemisphere. Even the New East Coast inside the Appalachians was slowing down.

"What am I looking at here?" Elias said. "Somebody talk sense to me."

"Says Mr. I-Designed-the-System."

"Not the time, Fiver."

"Check the elements list, Chief," Bigwig said. "I see all the usual programs, and then there's an extra one at the bottom: BlackRabbit. What the hell is *BlackRabbit*?"

"Doesn't sound great," Fiver said.

"Indeed, it doesn't," Elias said. "Have you guys seriously still not read the book?"

"You're the chief." Fiver sounded genuinely pissed. "All this comes from you."

"Not this," Elias said. "Must be a foreigner in the system."

"A foreigner who created a new *element*?" Bigwig said. "No way. Nobody gets that deep on my watch."

"Well, apparently, they do." Fiver said. "Blueberry, what do you think?"

"I'm seeing what you're seeing," Blueberry said. "I'll try to get under it. Figure out where it crawled up from."

Elias gripped the arms of his chair. Lonely at the top, but that just meant it was time to be the boss again. "Do that," he said. "In the meantime, Bigwig, I want you to run some nasty OWSLAFA code on this thing and kill it. Use KEHAAR too if you have to. I don't care if you derail the system for an hour. We can put the pieces back together before opening bell in NNYC. Fiver, we're going to run on Efrafa Protocol until then. Code Woundwort. Money's hardly moving anyway. I'll send a smokescreen message out to the markets. Should keep everyone from losing their shit for at least an hour. I don't know how this thing got in here, but it needs to be gone pronto. Nobody should be able to break us this bad. Understood?"

"Understood," Bigwig offered.

No one else chorused.

Elias stood up to pace. He needed movement to think, and the silence overhead told him everyone was doing their jobs. BlackRabbit? Where in the wide, weird world of coding had *that* come from? Of course, he remembered the Black Rabbit from the novel. How could he forget? Easily the scariest character he'd ever come across as a skinny little kid reading under the covers in Nebraska. But now Nebraska was no more, was just a smoking hole surrounding the remains of Omaha, and he'd been very intentional in not including anything Black Rabbit-related when building the Inlé System. Why would he? The Black Rabbit meant only one thing, and it was not good.

"Hey, Hazel?" Fiver again. "Sorry to bug, but we just lost the eastern seaboard—in case you didn't notice."

"Okay," Hazel muttered. "Got it. Thanks."

"And Hazel?"

"Yeah?"

"Sorry about being a dick earlier. All for one, and one for all, right?"

"Sure. Let me know when you figure something out."

"Will do."

Elias paced. *All for one, and one for all.* Funny how both true and not true that was. It wasn't a productive thought, especially not in the middle of what was becoming a bona fide crisis, but he couldn't help but think about the people below. A thousand smoke dwellers. A million ash chokers. Countless deeply fried-out and fucked-up consumers. They wouldn't know any of this was going on, but, if the markets *did* crash, their shitty lives were going to get a lot shittier.

"Hazel?"

Bigwig sounded tense.

"Yeah-huh?"

"I just ran everything we got, and Mr. BlackRabbit has not budged."

"OWSLA and OWSLAFA?"

"Affirmative."

"KEHAAR too?"

"Yes, sir. Money's pretty much stopped everywhere now. You get that cover message out to the markets?"

"Shit. Forgot."

"No worries, Chief. You still got ... ten minutes before Europe goes live."

"Got to go."

"Cool. I'll keep trying t—"

Bigwig's growl cut off abruptly, and Elias looked up at the ceiling. Just that same, fine-ass wood, but losing his head of security mid-sentence was not an encouraging sign. He slid back into his seat and waved up his screen. "Fiver?" he called. "Fiver, you there? I just lost Bigwig. Something up with the feed?"

"Looking into it, Boss ... Uh-oh."

"What?"

"East coast is black."

"I know the system went down. Shouldn't affect Bigwig's comm."

"No. It's not just *dark*. It's *black*—like no fucking power up and down the seaboard."

"Not possible."

"Run your own diagnostic."

"Diagnostics monitor the system, Fiver, not the power grid. That's a government thing."

A slight but knowing pause from above.

"You really telling me the system can't access government stuff?" Fiver said. "You really expect me to believe *that*?"

Elias blew out a long sigh. He needed to calm down. He needed to focus. He needed to be the *chief*. "Look. Do we have that kind of capability? I'm not saying *yes*. I'm not saying *no*. But, believe me when I also say that, if I keep secrets from you, it's for your own protection, Little Buddy."

"Think we're beyond that now, *Big Buddy*. Europe's trying to go live as we speak. From what I can see on the boards, there is a *great deal* of consternation about why no one can find their money."

"Fuck! I never sent the tech message."

"Pull it together, Chief."

"Got to go—"

"Has to be Holly time now, right? Everything from New Boston to Nueva Miami is going to be burning in an hour. Let's get some boots on the ground."

"To do what? We still don't even know what this thing is, let alone where it's coming from."

"Then send them to my place. We'll probably go dark next. Sorry, I mean *black*."

"We're not going to go dark, Fiver, let alone *black*. The local system's so fortified you couldn't squeeze a hair in."

"Which would be more reassuring if BlackRabbit wasn't *already inside the system*."

"You really think it's doing all this?"

"You just said the system can hack the grid."

"No. I only *implied* it, and the North American grid is still pretty resilient. This isn't Australia."

"Said all the Australians circa '36."

"Don't be an alarmist."

"Thought that's what you were paying me for?"

"Then don't make me stop paying you."

"Sorry, Chief. Just getting a little nervous. A lot of angry Luddies up here in the Bay. A lot of disgruntled, antisocial folks who'd just love to get a piece of my fuzzy ass."

"Not going to happen, my friend. Going now. Stay crunchy."

"As if there were any other way."

Elias fired off the usual boilerplate tech difficulties message with two minutes to spare. He should have done it twenty minutes ago. Really, he should have done it as soon as Asia went dark. He was slipping. Getting complacent.

"Hey, Chief?"

Blueberry. Thank God!

"Got something you should hear."

"Go ahead," Elias said, struggling again to breathe deep. At least the Whiz Kid was still on board.

"Been doing some digging, and our new friend BlackRabbit is not exactly what it appears to be."

"Go on—quickly if possible."

"It's not really an element in the system. Not even a foreign one. It's more like—how do I put this?—*under* the system, if that makes sense."

"It doesn't, but I'm still listening."

"Well, when you wrote the code for the Inlé System, you used universal basic, right?"

"I hardly even wrote it. I just slammed together a bunch of shit that already existed. I'm not exactly a visionary on that front, as you well know. Just a guy who understands that wealthy people like to get their money quickly."

"Right. Which is why you probably don't know that universal basic still stems from somewhere—a kind of Ur-language known only to eighty-year-old former Micro employees."

"*What* language?"

"Never mind, Chief. Whatever this thing is, it's operating on that ancient level. That's what I mean by *underneath* the system. You could also say it's like inside the *inside* of the system. Point being, we don't have any way to stop it short of pulling the plug."

"Like how the plug just got pulled on the east coast?"

"Yeah, but even that only slowed it for a sec. You would not believe how creaky the languages on some of the old government servers are. We're talking the digital equivalent of Sanskrit. Some are on fusion generators that are still firing, and that's where this thing seems to be based."

"Can you find them? I can send in Holly's boys if need be. They can fuck a server up right quick."

"Negative. Those puppies are bunkered so far underground the new governments don't even know where they are. That's why the power usually stays on when everything else goes to shit."

"But not this time?"

"Correct."

"Because BlackRabbit doesn't *want* it to stay on?"

"So it would seem."

"No bueno."

"No, indeed. It also means we've got maybe ... ten minutes before BlackRabbit overwhelms the local digit-bots and shuts us down too."

"You mean shuts *you* down in Alabamia? Or *me* here in the Sunshine State?"

"Shuts us *all* down, Chief. You need to alert the markets."

"Oh, they are going to *love* that."

"Is what it is, Boss."

"But why's it coming for *us*? I mean, it's called *BlackRabbit* for fuck's sake. That can't be a coincidence."

"Guess whoever it is—*whatever* it is—read the book."

"Guess they did. You know what the Black Rabbit is, right? ... Blueberry? ... You still there? ... Hello? ... *Hello!*"

Elias checked his screen. Everything east of the Mississippi Gorge was now dark. Well, shit. There goes the Whiz Kid. Then again, if it was just a matter of minutes before this thing overwhelmed the whole system, then he just needed to be ready to be overwhelmed. It was that simple. Step one was alerting the markets—or whatever was left of them. Maybe he could even spin it as something planned, some kind of in-house drill all-powerful Inlé was running. No one outside the team really knew how the system worked anyway. Everyone would just have to hunker and deal.

A chill licked the base of Elias's spine. More a bad feeling than an actual idea. Surely, he had not been so foolish as to ...

"Hey, Fiver," he said as calmly as possible. "Quick question for you, Buddy."

"Fire away, Chief—assuming you know we just lost Blueberry."

"That's sort of what I'm wondering about. When we reconfigured the security ground-bots last year. We used the system, right?"

"As we always do."

"Uh-huh. And, when we did, we un-linked them back so they could still run independent, didn't we?

"Uhh."

"*Didn't we?*"

"If I recall, it came down to a question of cost efficiency—"

"Mother*fuck!* Tell Holly to scramble strike forces A, B, and C. I want A and B surrounding my complex asap. You can have C at your place."

"Come on. You don't really think—"

"Do it now, Fiver."

"System's starting to sketch out over the Sierras ..."

"I repeat, get Holly's birds in the air *now*. We're about to go *black*—like, full-on, no-power, the-Luddies-are-going-to-come-for-our-balls *black*."

A heavy silence above.

"Wow," Fiver said finally. "Never thought this day would come ... and yet, somehow, I always knew it would."

"Don't get fatalistic. We're going to be fine. Just get the cavalry in the air."

"Told you I had a bad feeling, didn't I?"

"Yes, and it was duly noted."

"Hazel?"

"Yeah?"

"I love you, man."

"Do your job, Fiver!"

But Elias was only talking to the ceiling. He didn't know how he knew. He just *knew*, and the dark wall that had taken the place of his screen only confirmed it. Too bad he hadn't bothered to say *I love you* back to his closest approximation of a friend. Also, too bad he hadn't used his final few seconds of comm power to call Holly himself. It shouldn't matter though. Protocol in case of a system-wide crash was to get boots around the chief pronto. That went double for an actual implosion of the grid. Either way, all he had to do was sit tight and wait for the sound of some very expensive gunships to come pinwheeling down on his position. Sadly, Fiver and company could not depend on a similar rescue, but, worse come to worse, he could always hire more talent. At least a full system crash would also purge BlackRabbit.

He slumped in his chair. The study had gone dark. Even the complex generator was hooked into the system. *Stupid!* He tipped back and considered the now black ceiling above him. Sucker had cost a fortune! But so had this whole place. Cliffside complexes high above ongoing metro fires didn't grow on non-existent trees. But just how high was that cliff anyway? More importantly, how long would it take any would-be Luddie martyrs to scale it in pursuit of his head? Probably at least half an hour. Probably. Should be more than enough time for the choppers to get here ...

His screen blinked to life. For a second, his brain couldn't accept this. It couldn't be on, not without any power. But it was, and it was showing him something very different than the normal Inlé System monitoring visual. Instead of the usual colorful flow of digitized dollars, he was looking at some kind of twisty nest of dark tunnels. They looked cold, and they looked deep, and something was echoing out at him from each one. It took another second to recognize these sounds for what they were, and yet another to verify that the sound was muted on his screen. It didn't matter. They continued to fill the cool, carefully filtered air no longer circulating around his head.

Screams. Each of the tunnels was emitting a scream.

"What the—?"

"*Hazel,*" a frigid voice said from deep within the tunnels. "*Hazel, I'm calling you.*"

"I—" he sat frozen in his chair. "Who am I talking to?"

"*No one can deny me, Hazel. When I call, you must come.*"

"I—I don't understand."

"*I think you do, Hazel. I think you've understood ever since you were a child.*"

"Who is this? Fiver? You fucking with me? Because now is *not* the time—"

"*Hazel, I'm calling you. The thousand are at your door.*"

"The *what*? Listen, I don't know who you are, or what you want. But, I promise you, I am no fucking *rabbit*, and, when I *do* find out who you are, I will personally—"

"*You will see me soon enough, Hazel. I will meet you in my coldest, darkest burrow.*"

"We'll see about that!"

The screen disappeared, and the study fell back into darkness. Elias sprang up from his chair, but there was nowhere to go. He was all alone in his inner sanctum, and that was the safest place he could be. But what was up with that *voice?*—like the book had come to life! No. Just one very specific part of it ... the terrifying part. And where were those choppers! Holly's boys should be here by now. They should be raining down to protect their chief, to save him from ... from ...

Thud! Something heavy crashed against the study door. It sounded like a tire iron, or maybe the spikey end of a torn-off table leg. *Thud!* It hit again, and the bolt rattled above the handle. It was an electric bolt, which meant it was also dead, was just a thin, dumb piece of metal that couldn't hold for long.

"*Hazel,*" the cold voice filled the darkness. "*I am looking forward to our meeting.*"

Thud! There were voices in the hall outside the door. Many voices. Angry voices. The enraged shrapnel babble of a thousand claws scraping against each other.

Elias waved his hands frantically through the dark, but no screen materialized. "What do you want from me?" he screamed.

"*I think you know.*"

"Don't take me. Please. I'll do anything!"

"*Hazel, it's time for you to come home.*"

"No! Please!"

Thud! The door crashed down, and the burning world streamed inside.

Wesley Stine

Jacob's Ladder

Jacob

THE MORE THAT I LOOK BACK on the events which I have seen in my days, and the adversities through which the Lord has seen fit to conduct me, the more I am convinced that 2156 was the most important year of my life.

I know full well that grown men making such claims about their childhoods (and I was only twelve years old at the time) are seldom taken seriously. But you must judge the story of Jacob Martin for yourself. And when you have read it, and really thought about it, I doubt that you will accuse me of indulging in an excess of sentimentality.

To begin with, you must understand that as a child I was very shy, perhaps shyer than all the other boys who lived between the two forks of the river Esconaba, where they meet at the town of Gwinn, in the land of Yuper. I cannot say that I had even a single friend until I was ten years old — for that was the age that I became friends with Felix.

Felix was a boy of medium size, moderately strong, with a cheery and earnest temperament. He was the eldest of three brothers, and they all had black hair and tawny skin; the latter was rare in Yuper, though if you go further south you will come to lands where almost everyone looks like Felix and his brothers. Felix had always tried earnestly to be the faithful friend of every other boy in Gwinn, even an awkward boy like myself — one who had hitherto ignored every other child outside his own family, not because he was happier being alone, but because the impulse to do otherwise had not yet been awakened.

But that was no obstacle to Felix, and I recall with great happiness the long afternoons that the two of us spent exploring the edges of the forests, and the hill country north of Gwinn. Often we hunted or snared small animals, or flew homemade kites, or searched for artifacts from earlier centuries, or played marbles, checkers, and darts.

Things which had before seemed dull to me ceased to be so when Felix was present. Sunday school, for instance—where I never learned anything that I did not already know from my private studies—no longer seemed like a waste of time.

Even my father the carpenter, who might have complained that little Jacob was too often away with Felix when he might have been at the workshop, seemed to be happy about what was happening—happy that his son was learning how not to be a loner.

Because there is not space here for me to fully relate my adventures with Felix, I will limit myself to describing one incident which to me seems especially notable.

One day, when we were both eleven years old, Felix and I were exploring near a place where it was said that military aircraft had once been kept. There we found a very curious piece of metal, about the length of our forearms. We brought it back to Gwinn, and along with my sister Sarah, we took it to Adam Fau, to see if he could identify it.

Adam Fau was, among other things, a collector of books. He had three or four hundred of them in his handsome log house, and you would not find a larger collection anywhere, unless you went downriver to Esky, or northward over the hills to Markét-on-Superior. He often let children such as myself borrow his books, in exchange for doing simple chores like spreading fresh straw in his henhouse, or polishing the mirror of his wife's solar cooker.

This annoyed some of the adults, for if their children remained interested in books as they grew older, then Mr. Fau would start requiring, and getting, more substantial trades. But my parents were not annoyed; indeed they were quite bookish themselves.

Anyway, after Felix and Sarah and I had examined our curious metal, we showed Mr. Fau its strange properties—how it was strong like steel but much lighter, and how it shone like silver if you polished it. He said that he did not know of any metal quite like it, but that if he later found mention of one in his books, he would tell us. And a few days later, he told us that he had learned that this light, strong, and shiny metal was called mithril, and that it was a good material for making armor.

Some time later, Felix and I brought our piece of mithril to Gwinn's blacksmith, who lived on the west fork of the Esconaba, right by the waterwheel that pumped the bellows in his forge. We asked him whether he would be able to make anything useful out of it, but no matter how hard he tried, he could find no way to work it, for the secret of shaping mithril had apparently been lost to the passing years.

This was only one of many things that Felix and I did together, for we were quite good friends. But you must understand that at this time, I was still for the most part solitary. I did not really have any friends apart from Felix, or any friends at all who shared my pensive disposition, and my love for ancient lore.

That changed early in 2156, when Enos Hartfeld arrived in the town of Gwinn.

Enos was born in a coastal town called Munising, and he lived there until his parents were drowned when their skiff went down in one of those storms that Lake Superior is so famous for. After this, Enos and his elder sister were sent to live with their aunt and uncle in Gwinn. Enos seemed, at most times, to be a cheerful boy, even after his parents' death, though I must admit that he might have been even more cheerful beforehand, without my knowing it. Yet what happened still seemed to have made him more contemplative.

Enos was fairly quiet (though not so quiet as myself) and he spent more time in church than any of the other boys. And whenever Reverend Toivonen went looking for youths to labor with him in the little vineyard behind the church where our communion wine was made, Enos was usually the first to volunteer. Though again, I must admit that I cannot know whether he was this religious by nature, or because of what he had experienced.

Enos was a little younger and smaller than myself. He had black hair and an owlish face, a light but agile build, and a beautiful voice. He was amiable and free of malice, though when the boys wrestled or fought for sport, Enos proved just as fierce as any of the others, and he was witty and incisive in all our verbal games. If he had any trait that the rest of us found annoying, it was that he too easily left us and our games behind when he felt that he was needed on the farm. Yet this dutifulness, I think, was not borne out of passivity; he simply disliked the thought that his aunt and uncle's lives might be made harder if their nephew was not around when they needed him.

Doubtless you are by now thinking of how strange it must be for a grown man to describe his childhood friend in such an ebullient manner. Tragedy, it is true, can cause us to exaggerate the beauty that came before, and I certainly did not think of Enos in quite these terms when I was actually with him. But the more that I reflect on those happy years we spent together, the more I am convinced that my characterization is, in the essentials, correct.

But I will return to my narrative. I think that the time I first realized what a good friend I had found in Enos came in the spring of 2156, when we were both twelve years old. Enos, like myself, frequently borrowed books from Mr.

Fau. In one of these books, he had apparently read a story about how Benjamin Franklin had invented electricity by petting cats backwards, and on one bright and cloudless Sunday morning, after the service was over, he was trying to impress some of the other boys by telling them this fact. Yet they all seemed indifferent, except for me.

"Benjamin Franklin invented electricity by pettings cats backward," said Enos.

"But can *we* make electricity by petting cats backward?" I said.

"Yes," said Enos. "That's what the sparks are, in the cat's fur. Electricity. Just like lightning is electricity."

"Everyone knows that cats make sparks," I said. "But not everyone knows that sparks are electricity."

And for a while, we did not know what to do to convince the others that we were right.

But then we started thinking about wires. Everyone knew that electricity was what ran through wires. (Gwinn's radioman, for instance, needed electricity, so he ran a wire to a little generator on the blacksmith's waterwheel.) Enos and I decided that if we could make the sparks from cats' fur run through a wire, then the others would believe us.

"You have cats," I said, "and I have wires."

It was true—Enos's aunt and uncle had a large supply of barn cats, and my father's workshop had a surplus of old wires, since salvage merchants were always finding wires faster than craftsmen like my father could find uses for them.

And so, later that same afternoon, Enos and I met in front of his house, where he supplied his fluffiest calico cat, and I supplied a length of copper wire. Soon we found that if one of us petted the cat backward, letting the little sparks of electricity build up with each stroke, then if we each touched one end of the wire, we would both get shocked.

Soon the word had spread of what we were up to, and other children were gathering around to find out if it was true. We let them all repeat the experiment for themselves, taking turns shocking and being shocked, until they were all convinced of Enos's claim that Benjamin Franklin had invented electricity by petting cats backward. And we all went away feeling quite happy about what we had achieved—all of us except for the cat.

Enos and I were quite close after that, though Felix remained as important to me as ever, and it was at about this same time that the three of us became good friends with Miles.

Miles had hair the color of sand, and he was very tall; at the age of twelve he had already passed some of Gwinn's grown men in height. He had stretch marks on his back from growing so fast, and if you saw Miles in the sauna or at the swimming hole you might have thought that he was being whipped at home, if you did not know his parents.

The winter that he was fourteen, Miles enjoyed a few days of local fame for the calmness with which he conducted himself after he broke his arm while out lumbering—how he did not cry when it happened, how he instructed his little brother in the method of making a splint, and how he harnessed his horse and drove his sled homeward over the snow with his good arm, not even abandoning his load of timber.

But in 2156, all of that lay in the future, and Miles, though the tallest of us, was very much a child—a freckle-faced, restless, and jocular child.

For the four of us—myself, Enos, Felix, and Miles—there could scarcely have been a happier time than the summer of 2156. We were nearly inseparable. When Enos and I went to Adam Fau's house to read adventure stories like *Starship Troopers* and *The Hobbit* and *Johnny Tremain*, Felix and Miles joined us, and after a while they found themselves enjoying the books almost as much as we did. And you can imagine how pleased Reverend Toivonen must have been when Enos, instead of appearing by himself on mornings when the church vineyard was in need of work, came as head of a company of four.

The best times of all came during those long, hot afternoons when we all managed to finish our chores early enough to go swimming. Sometimes other boys joined us—Vance and Ilmari, most often—but on many days it was just myself and Felix and Enos and Miles who crossed the rushing Esconaba and clambered uphill for nearly a mile to the spot where the cold mountain stream turned into a swimming hole that was wonderfully broad and deep.

We spent so many hours naked in that place that we came to know it as well as we knew our own farms—from the little waterfall at the head of the pool, to the low rock cliff that was perfect for diving, and from the long lane where we sometimes raced, to the deep, pebble-strewn bottom where boys who were good at holding their breath sometimes found ancient coins. Nor were we any less familiar with the minutiae of the surrounding forest, its trees and shrubs and butterflies and birds.

Miles, Felix, and I had grown up knowing two strokes. Enos knew two others, which he taught us; he had learned them (along with the first two) in Munising, which, like most harbor towns, had a schoolmaster who instructed his pupils in swimming along with the other subjects. Nonetheless, out of the four of us Miles was the strongest swimmer, easily prevailing in any contest into which he put his full effort. But this was hardly surprising for someone so tall that the rest of us could stand immersed nearly chest deep in water that only came up to his belly button.

Even after our skin had been numbed in the frigid water, we kept up our games with as much zeal as before. It was only when we had worn out every last muscle that we pulled ourselves out of the water and began to dry our bodies under the pleasant rays of the westering sun.

Then, for a good long time, we lay limply on the stony bank, still naked, though in the cold water our dangling bits had shriveled almost to nothing. If we were not too tired, we might play the riddle game, until the lengthening shadows which the pine trees cast over the water told us that it was time to dress and head for home.

On some days, instead of trying to answer ordinary riddles like the other boys, Enos and I would riddle each other with numbers. We took turns thinking of a sequence and saying its first few terms aloud; you answered the riddle by finding the number that came next.

One time, I lay there reflecting on how, in my father's carpentry shop, we often had to divide something in half over and over again, and then take just one piece away, leaving the others. So for my sequence, I said "One, three, seven, fifteen, thirty-one."

I thought that it would take Enos a long time to figure it out, but it didn't. "Sixty-three," he said. "It's doubles minus one."

Then it was Enos's turn: "Seven, four, eleven, fifteen, twenty-six, forty-one."

I spent more time on this sequence than he had on mine, but after a while I was sure I had the answer. "Sixty-seven," I said. "It's the Fibonacci numbers, just like Mr. Moser taught us. Only instead of starting with one and two, you started with seven and four."

And that, of course, was the answer. But the trouble with the number game was that, when we really got to understanding just how many different things you can do with numbers, the game suddenly became much more difficult.

I recall quite clearly that on the last day we played this game (and by that time we were well beyond merely toying with primes and composites and the like), I had given Enos the sequence: "Two, six, twelve, twenty, thirty."

And for a long time he did not answer, but seemed lost in deep thought. I was worried that I had ruined the game, because Enos might well puzzle over a thing like that for what seemed like a million years rather than give up, but at last he spoke. "The answer," he said, "is forty-two."

Then, a moment later: "Those numbers are like squares, only instead of multiplying a number by itself, you multiply it by the number after it."

And then Enos took his turn, saying: "One, two, six, twelve, sixty, sixty, four hundred and twenty."

I thought and thought about what the answer might be, but I made no progress—not while I lay there by the swimming hole, and not in the days and weeks afterward, as I kept contemplating it in my idle moments. Even when I had enlisted the help of my sister Sarah, the problem continued to stump both of us.

When so much time had passed that we felt like Enos would not mind, Sarah and I asked Mr. Fau whether he thought it was a real sequence, or whether Enos might have just been pulling my leg.

"He was almost certainly pulling your leg," said Mr. Fau. "Not only did he repeat the number sixty, which should not have been necessary, but that last number, four hundred and twenty, has a double meaning. When the people who were old when I was born were youngsters themselves, they used 'four-twenty' as a code name for a weed which some of the more rebellious ones smoked for pleasure."

After that, several years went by in which I hardly ever thought about the number game at all, until a certain day when I was working at carpentry with my father, and my thoughts turned to the various measuring devices in our workshop.

When you purchase your tools from salvage merchants, they do not come in the matching sets in which they were made. Thus, a carpenter must get used to switching back and forth between different scales of measure—one based on tens, and another on twos and fours and sixes and twelves. Tens are easier to do math with, but for some reason it was the system of twelves, with its feet and inches and half- and quarter-inches, which felt the most natural when I was working with my hands.

I started wondering if this was because you can divide twelve by one, two, three, or four and get whole numbers. You can't do that with ten, or with any other number less than twelve. Though if you only need to divide by one, two, and three, then a group of six will do, and to divide by one and two, you only need a group of two. And these were the proportions my father and I most often chose to work with, when we had to decide for ourselves how to measure and cut our workpiece.

Then I remembered that the same people who had divided the foot into twelve inches had also divided the hour into sixty minutes. The upshot was that an hour, besides being divisible in all the ways that a foot was divisible, could also be split into fifths. Or sixths—you did not need to go any higher to get a number divisible by everything from one to six. And these numbers—one, two, six, twelve, sixty, and sixty again—were the beginning of Enos's sequence!

Only one loose end remained. After a few minutes of intense cogitation, I had found the smallest common multiple of all the numbers from one to seven, and it was four hundred and twenty. Mr. Fau had been wrong. Enos was not pulling my leg after all, and his final number had nothing to do with smoking weeds for pleasure.

By this time, my father had noticed that I was working quite slowly, and he asked if something was the matter. I said that I was alright, and I scolded myself for falling behind, and I made sure to complete the rest of that day's work with more than my usual diligence. We were making an ox-yoke at the time, an intricate task in which my father had only recently decided I was ready to assist. And that was something of which I felt quite proud.

But I must not get too far ahead of myself. The tall, broad-shouldered youth who made ox-yokes and measured his growing skill in the trade against his father's was quite a different Jacob Martin than the scrawny twelve-year-old who worked when he had to, but who otherwise cared far more about swimming, and the riddle game, and the secrets of Mr. Fau's books.

In due time, the summer of 2156 came to an end. It had been a good summer — one of those long, hot summers which the elders say were never seen as far north as Yuper before the present century — but eventually, the sun retreated into the south, the days became shorter, and the season changed to autumn.

Felix and Enos and Miles and I remained close that autumn, though not quite as close as before. Partly this was because autumn was the season for football, and while Miles was an excellent lineman, and Felix was a passable wide receiver, Enos and I had no talent for that game at all.

Winter and Christmas brought another flurry of happy memories, for in between singing carols and celebrating the Lord's birth, the four of us found plenty of time to exert ourselves to the utmost in winter amusements.

Often we steamed ourselves in the sauna together, before the heat became too much to bear and we rushed out to roll naked in the snow. Many a wild toboggan ride down the slopes of the northern bluffs left us frightened nearly out of our wits, and on the last day of school before the holiday, we relied on Miles' firm leadership to prevail in a schoolyard snowball fight against a foe twice as numerous as ourselves.

These, alas, would be the last of our moments together. Early in the spring of 2157, Felix took ill of pneumonia. For seven days he was laid up in his bed, and on the eighth day he died.

It seemed that all of Gwinn had crowded into our little church for the funeral, and I do not think I can recall any sight as pitiful as that of Felix's two brothers, aged only nine and six, standing beside the bier in their best attire, and trying so earnestly to look the part of men. Reverend Toivonen preached a sermon on Christ's parable of the laborers in the Master's vineyard, and how each of them, whether the hours of his service were short or long, received the same reward, so long as he served the Lord of the Vineyard with all his heart.

These were comforting words, for we were all minded to believe that Felix had loved God and his neighbor with all his heart, soul, and mind. Yet near the end, the reverend also said something less agreeable, when he told us not to attach too much importance to either Felix's death or our own survival, since in the Lord's time, all men's lives are like the grass that soon withers away. The day was not long in coming when each of us would stand nearer to life's end than to its beginning, and when that day came, we too would think that all of life was but a brief moment.

Yet however trite this notion may have seemed back then, especially to a youngster burying one of his friends for the first time, all that I can say of it now, as I look back on those moments from the vantage point of middle age, is "How true that is!"

As great as my grief may have been at the time, I was still only a child, and I would soon return to my usual cheery temperament, just as Enos had done the previous year, after he lost his parents.

Enos and Miles and I remained fast friends, and all throughout that spring, and the beginning of the next summer, we worked through our chores with a sense of great urgency, for we did not wish to miss a single moment when the three of us might be together, whether that meant playing ball with the other boys, or joining them at the swimming hole, or mending Mr. Fau's garden fences in exchange for the privilege of borrowing books about sailing, or architecture, or zoology, or astronomy, or a certain group of twelve long-dead men who had climbed inside rockets and flown to the moon.

This continued until a certain day in June, when Enos was sent away from Gwinn by his aunt and uncle to tend sheep.

The family had purchased grazing rights on some meadows in the uplands eleven miles northwest of Gwinn, halfway to the village of Ishming. Their plan was that, as soon as the lambs were large enough, Enos would take the flock of forty-nine ewes and nearly as many lambs to graze there for ten weeks, before returning them to the family farm in Gwinn.

Each night, Enos was to sleep in a little hut beside the sheep pen and the shallow pond where the sheep were watered, and each day, he was to lead them over the lightly wooded hills in search of fresh grass.

To me, all of this came as a great disappointment, since it meant that I would not be seeing my friend in all of that time. Yet the prevailing mood among the people of Gwinn was one of happiness for the Hartfeld family—happiness that they had found a way to expand their flock of sheep, and happiness that they had a boy who was active and diligent enough to be entrusted with such a task. Indeed, there was even speculation at that time over which girl would be lucky enough to have Enos as her husband when he came of age—a detail which, when I look back on it, only makes the story I am telling even more bitter.

Enos's departure to tend the flock that summer marked the end of his time as my best friend. I grew closer to other boys during his absence, and even after he returned in September, autumn and football drew us yet further apart, for I had improved since the last year and could now play a decent safety, while Enos remained as inept as ever. After another year passed, and Enos had returned from the sheepfold twice, he seldom joined Miles and me at the swimming hole or at Mr. Fau's house, and he seldom asked us to join him at Reverend Toivonen's vineyard.

I must warn you that the way I am relating these events is not the same— indeed cannot be the same—as the way I experienced them. When you are a child, and another child does not try to play with you as often as before, you do not think long and hard about why this might be. You simply find different children to play with.

One year, my best friend was Felix. Two years later, it was Enos, and then Miles, and then Ilmari, and then Joel. And after that I was courting a girl. Except for Felix, I put almost no thought into the reasons why each of these friends had been displaced. And it was only through the hard school of experience that I later grew into the kind of person who was thoughtful enough to make such a list at all.

Twelve-year-old Jacob would have been shocked if he could peer into the future and see that fifteen-year-old Enos had no interest at all in Mr. Fau's books. But fifteen-year-old Jacob was not. Children's interests changed as they grew up; this was natural and occurred to some degree with everyone, and since it was Sarah and Ilmari who were most often my reading companions at that later time, it was Sarah and Ilmari whom I thought of when I thought of books.

And all of my boyhood amusements, of whatever sort, were with time sub- sumed beneath a simple satisfaction in taking on more and more of the duties that came with manhood, and in the sense of respect that followed in their train.

I remember well the day when my father told me that he had heard that a salvage merchant in Markét-on-Superior had gotten ahold of two valuable bubble levels, and was looking for buyers for them. He gave me a large sum of silver and sent me off all by myself to journey twenty-two miles overland and bid for one of them. And to be entrusted with a responsibility like that brought me far more happiness than I could have gotten by hanging out with my friends, which was as it should be—one cannot be a child forever.

Even so, I cannot but feel at least some guilt that I did not speak with Enos more often in our final years of boyhood. I should have noticed how much his temperament had changed—how (despite some attempts to hide it) he had become more remote and irritable than I would ever have expected. Of course, nothing that I did, or did not do, could have mattered much in the long run, but still, Enos deserved better from me.

There is one other thing of which I must make note, before I continue my tale. It is that, during these years, Enos became quite sickly, and did not grow as much as the other boys did, leaving his aunt and uncle to fear that he might always be stunted. Though at the time, I did not see any connection between this and the other things that I will soon relate.

Most of what I now know of Enos's character during those later years came only second- and third-hand, from things that I heard after his departure from Gwinn, when rumor with her thousand tongues set out to make the whole town aware of just what kind of lad it was that we had lost.

Enos, it was said, was an idler. He slept too much and had to be prodded to keep up with his chores. Any farm task which his uncle entrusted to him was likely to be done shoddily. And while he made a show of dutifully taking the sheep up into the hills each year for their summer grazing, his neglect always became apparent when the flock returned in much worse health than it had gone out.

The reason that Enos had few friends was because he was ill-tempered, stubborn, and greedy. He was also irreligious — not only had he completely given up his childhood habit of working with Reverend Toivonen in the vineyard, he had also ceased all scripture-reading and other private devotions. His family had to threaten him to get him to attend Sunday services, and in private he would often speak in such crude and blasphemous tones that you would doubt he had spent even half his life in the pious land of Yuper.

Enos was a wastrel; his aunt and uncle had had to lock up their supply of cider and other liquors to keep him from imbibing them on the sly. And he was — or at least, he tried to be — a rake; Cammy Howe, the girl who had loved Enos with a love kindled in his earlier days, was now talking about how rudely he had berated her when she resisted his attempts to lead her into indecent acts.

The event which occasioned this cascade of rumors — in which all of Enos's faults were bruited about so publicly, and without which I would not have guessed at the severity of his decline — was as follows: When Enos and I were each eighteen years old, a company of miscreants arrived in our region of Yuper, a troupe of unruly men (and a few women) who had no homeland, but who wandered where they had to to stay ahead of the law, making their living by thievery, gambling, dealing in unlawful goods, and staging vulgar and licentious entertainments.

Gwinn's radioman warned us in advance of these travelers' reputation, and our mayor forbade them from entering his town. The mayor of Esky did likewise, and the vagrants were obliged to make camp in Cornell, a smaller but more tolerant village a little north of Esky.

Though both mayors tried to keep their citizens from stealing away to visit the vagrants' camp, their strictures proved impossible to enforce, and many of the gullible youths, along with the more dissolute among the older folk, took their turns frequenting the place.

While all of this was going on, my father and I were hard at work fitting out a new mill. We paid almost no attention to the storms of gossip all around us, and I might have quickly forgotten about the whole event, had news not arrived of how Enos Hartfeld had filched a substantial sum of money from his aunt and uncle, slunk away to attend the filthy show, and squandered the money on frivolities. Then, rather than return to Gwinn and face the consequences of his deeds, Enos had joined the vagrant troupe, vanishing alongside his new companions when they loaded their wagons early the next morning and took to the road.

There were, of course, different accounts of the particulars, yet they all agreed in the essentials. Some witnesses also claimed to have seen Enos in the company of two of the heavily painted stage women, late at night after their show was finished, performing acts not fit to be described.

Because these tidings came when my father and I were busy with the mill, I did not give them much immediate thought. But when the mill was finished, and I had time to reflect on what I had heard, I was filled with consternation.

I had never expected Enos to come to such an end as this, and I vacillated between being angry at the vagrants for ensnaring a boy who, whatever his faults, must have still had at least some light left in him, and being angry at myself, for paying so little attention to Enos over the years that I did not see him becoming the kind of youth who might be tempted by the vagrants.

Enos's family, though deeply dismayed at what had happened, did not appear surprised. After all, they had known him all throughout his long decline, while I had known him closely only when he was twelve, when he seemed like the last person in the world who would do what he later did.

Yet I also knew full well that people could change with the passage of years, and that the façade hiding a decrepit private life might crumble in a single moment. I had seen it happen on other occasions as I grew to manhood; Enos's case was simply more dramatic than most.

There were, in the meantime, still crops to be planted and harvested, barns to be raised, and trees to be felled, then hammered and sawed and sanded and steamed into all the tools that made our way of life possible. And there were songs to be sung, and dances to be danced, and christenings and weddings and funerals to be attended to.

At the end of the summer that followed Enos's disappearance, Miles (who was by now the tallest man in Gwinn) moved to Little Lake, four miles to the east, to marry. I was there with him for three days, eating and drinking and dancing and playing football and listening to fiddle music, and doing all the other things that the Yuper folk do when a boy and a girl tie the knot. After I had returned to Gwinn and caught up on my chores, I went to Mr. Fau's house late one September evening to return one book and borrow another.

Somehow — and I do not remember what it was in the books that had raised this topic — our conversation turned to the various toxins which had been strewn over the earth in earlier centuries.

"Sometimes you hear people say that radioactives are the worst," said Mr. Fau. "But it's just a myth. Most of the isotopes decayed a long time ago, and there were never any nuclear sites in Yuper to begin with. Heavy metals are a bigger deal anyway; they're just as poisonous, and they don't decay with time."

I asked Mr. Fau a question or two about heavy metals, and he told me that they had been used in mining and in other industries, and that some of them had been spilled quite carelessly into the environment, and that they're most likely to cause harm when they get dissolved in drinking water. People who drank from bad groundwater, or from small and shallow lakes or ponds, were at the greatest risk.

"If you ingest a lot of it," he said, "it can kill you. Otherwise it slowly makes you sicker. A lot of the time it degrades your brain. It can make a man go mad, or just get duller and meaner than he used to be."

This made me think of the handful of books I had read in which a character fell under the influence of a sorcerer's spell or a pharmacist's potion, and then — for a period that could last from minutes to years, depending on the needs of the plot — lived with his or her personality distorted, blinded to some emotions, while other were constantly inflamed.

When the author wanted to give his tale a happy ending, he would find a way for the spell to be broken. And then it was like waking up from one of those bad dreams where you've done things that would give your waking self cause to be ashamed, but then you realize, to your great relief, that they were not your own deeds at all.

I recalled the little pond in the place where Enos had kept his sheep. Early on, he had described it to me — it was about fifty feet long and thirty feet wide, and though he drank from it and bathed in it, it was no good for swimming, because the water only came up to his thighs.

Before hearing about heavy metals, I had been constrained to believe that, in the naiveté of childhood, I had misjudged Enos's character, or at least underestimated his natural capacity for change. But now I had seen a new explanation for his downfall, and I felt a burning desire to know the truth.

All that night, I could not sleep. In the morning, I rose before dawn, milked the cow, and then, from my father's workshop, I took a few strips of CHEMTRACE paper—paper which tuned different colors upon contact with different toxins, and which my father and I sometimes used to test salvaged goods. It could not detect every poison, but it could detect the most common ones.

I knelt and said the usual prayer for a safe journey, and then, by the light of the gibbous moon, I set out toward the place where Enos had kept his sheep for so many summers. It was easy to find, because it stood at the head of a creekbed which carried snowmelt in the springtime, but which was dry during the summer months, except after rainstorms.

A little before noon, I laid eyes on Enos's deserted hut. I ran to the edge of the pond, leaping over the sheep fence on the way, and dipped a CHEMTRACE strip into the placid water, where it slowly turned a pale blue. And blue, according to the strips' instruction card, meant "heavy metals."

Then, somewhat recklessly, I stripped off my trousers and waded down into the water, looking for the contamination's source. Among the large rocks on the far end of the pond, I saw something, mostly buried beneath the surrounding stones, which did not appear quite natural. Looking more closely, I saw that it was the exposed part of a badly rusted barrel. In it was a thin crack like a human hair, crisscrossed with ghostly filaments of corrosion.

I dipped another CHEMTRACE strip into the water above the barrel, and watched as it turned a deep, vivid blue.

A moment later I was out of the water, tramping back toward Gwinn, hardly paying attention to my own steps, and stumbling sometimes in the midst of my frenzied thoughts.

It was such a painful thing, to think of that bright and cheerful and innocent boy having his personality slowly erased. To think of his innermost feelings, so pure in the beginning, being lost in a haze of base passions, as (unbeknownst to him) he came back from the sheepfold each year with more and more of the of the invisible fibers of his mind either broken or missing. And to think of his growing blindness, not to the mere visible world, but to his own former desires—his desires to make and keep friends, to learn from books about the world beyond Gwinn, to work hard on his aunt and uncle's farm, to live an honest and chaste and upright life, and to worship Jesus his Savior.

With my own mind wracked by these thoughts, I could not travel at anywhere near my usual speed. A journey that should have only taken until about four o'clock instead lasted almost until sunset, when, at the very edge of town, I wandered somewhat aimlessly onto the farm of Anna Corcoran, Adam Fau's sister. Then, overcome with exhaustion (for I had not slept in a long time), I wandered beneath a ladder that was leaning up against Mrs. Corcoran's barn, and there I fell asleep, resting my tear-stained face on a pair of large rocks.

I slept soundly, through sunset and dusk and all throughout the night until the rosy-fingered dawn awoke me, and cleared away the weariness from my mind the way that only the first gentle sunbeams of morning ever can.

I stretched myself in the daylight, then leaned for a while against the ladder, as I began to remember where I was, and what I had been up to, and what dreadful things I now knew had happened to Enos over the last six years. But I also remembered that I had proven his spiritual innocence, and that however hopeless his earthly situation might be, in the long run there was nothing to fear. And then, as if bidden from on high, I rose up, shook the dust from off myself, left the ladder and Anna Corcoran's farm behind me, and walked briskly back to my own house.

My father, when he saw me coming, made as if to scold me for being absent all day and all night without a reason. But then he saw my disheveled appearance, and how my eyes were sore from so much crying, and he simply asked me what was the matter.

I explained everything. My father listened patiently, looking thoughtful and only seldom interrupting.

"That rusting barrel has me worried," he said. "It's only got a small leak now, but it'll get worse. If it ever bursts open and pours out all at once ..."

"Then what happened to Enos will happen to everyone," I said.

I had not yet thought about it, but if the accursed barrel somehow burst, then as soon as the next rainstorm hit, the creek would carry its toxins into the Esconaba, poisoning all of Gwinn.

And so, later that morning, we gathered four men—myself, my father, Sarah's fiancé, and his father—and headed back up to the old sheep pond with a handcart, several crowbars, and our thickest pairs of gloves. There, we lifted the rocks from around the barrel, then lifted the barrel itself, carted it back with us, and dumped it in an unclean place outside the boundaries of Gwinn.

At this time, nobody else knew our secret; we did not wish to raise a panic, and so we avoided talking about the noxious barrel until a man arrived in our town who knew what to do with it.

Herman Becerra made his annual visit to Gwinn late that fall, while my father and I were harvesting the cider apples. As a recent initiate in the Order of Afterlings, Herman was the nearest thing to a scientist that any of us would ever see.

(The Afterlings got their name because they view themselves as being the rearguard of a long scientific tradition; their mission is to do their best to prevent the more useful bits of mankind's knowledge from being lost to the ravages of time.)

My father and I told Herman what we knew, and after examining and test-ing the leaky barrel, Herman announced that it was *methylmercury* that had poisoned Enos.

"It was probably there," he said, "because the people in the twenty-first cen-tury had been using it for mining. They had ways to safely dispose of chemicals like methylmercury, but they involved a lot of money and red tape. So near the end, when law and order were breaking down, they started burying their waste shallowly, or leaving it to the elements."

Soon, the entire town had been notified of our discovery. The mayor, want-ing to get what was left of the toxic metal as far from Gwinn as he could, pro-vided Herman with a boat to take it downriver to Lake Michigan, and thence to Ñork, where there were men who knew how to transform it into a harmless red gemstone called cinnabar.

Among those who now knew the truth about Enos's downfall were his aunt and uncle. I can only imagine that they felt an even stronger version of what I felt — intense grief at what had been done to their nephew, mingled with a glimmer of relief that he was, in some sense, still innocent.

On at least two occasions, Enos's uncle left Gwinn to search for him, and he also sent messages by radio to some relatives in Sault Sainte Marie to be on the lookout for a short, frail, black-haired young man, possibly going by the name of "Enos," travelling with a company of degenerate showman.

They never did find him. Yet if they had, it was still anyone's guess whether they could have persuaded him to return. For all that we knew, the other vagrants had convinced him that his long mental decline was actually a journey of self-discovery, and that he did not need any healing at all.

(In truth, his family could only have offered him forgiveness, not healing — Herman Becerra had been quite blunt with us when he said that the effects of methylmercury ingestion during childhood were beyond all human power to reverse. For Enos, there could be no healing on this side of Gabriel's horn.)

Yet by this time there was really no knowing what had become of Enos. Perhaps he was still with those wandering degenerates, but perhaps they had determined that being dissolute did not on its own make him useful, and had dumped him somewhere along their circuit. Perhaps he had gotten himself killed in a quarrel. Perhaps he was wasting away of a venereal disease. And perhaps he had run afoul of the law and been imprisoned, or even hanged.

☉

When Herman Becerra made my discovery public, I briefly became the most respected man in Gwinn. The whole town seemed to have risen up in praise of me, and everyone was eager to find new ways to honor the ingenious young man who had preserved them from a grave danger.

But I found their praises irksome, and wished most of all to be treated like an ordinary youth—to be left alone so that I could cry and pray and mourn in peace. I, after all, had contributed only a few days of labor to the discovery; it was Enos who, though perfectly innocent, had suffered for the sins of a long-dead civilization, Enos who had lost everything.

But even that seemed like an understatement, for usually, when we speak of losing everything, we think only of dying, like Felix did. But while Felix's life was short, it was at least his own. He died young, but he died as himself.

Not so for Enos, whose mind had been disfigured beyond recognition, and who, I must suppose, went on to fritter away his days doing things which the younger Enos would have found contemptible, and which, even in his broken state, were doomed to bring him no lasting happiness.

The only people who seemed to really understand me at this time, and who did not try to assuage my grief by praising my own virtues, were my father and Reverend Toivonen.

The reverend often sat beside me quietly during those days, saying only a few words. And when he did speak, it was with words of comfort rather than flattery.

"I reckon that it will be well with him at the last day," he said. "The Lord has always been merciful to those who sin unwittingly."

Then, after a long silence: "You're probably thinking, 'Why did it have to be Enos? Why did it have to be someone so good?' But it's always the unblemished lamb that gets sacrificed. If we hadn't lost such a fine young man as him—if that horrid barrel had only poisoned some common youth, who didn't have as far to fall—then it would still be rusting away in that lake, because you wouldn't have been spurred to action.

"The shedding of innocent blood," he said a while later, "is a bitter price for mankind's sins. But there are times when it's the only price that can be paid."

My father, too, knew how to mourn with me when I mourned. He did not take umbrage when, all through that snowy winter, I wept from time to time in the midst of my labors in the workshop, nor did he allow merrymaking in his house when he could tell from my countenance that I was not yet ready for it.

"Herman Becerra told us that the people in the old days did this for money," I once said to him, rather plaintively. "To save money, because just abandoning their garbage was cheaper than dealing with it properly. How could—how could any amount of money be worth what that barrel did? What it did to Enos, how it—how it destroyed him?! They had to have known there was at least a chance of all that mercury seeping out—

"What did they think of all us people who hadn't been born yet? Did they care what happened to us? Why did they act like Enos—like we—like our lives were so cheap?"

"I suppose," said my father, "that they decided that since there was no one around back then to speak for us, it didn't matter what happened to us."

And that was the last that we talked about it for a long time, because there was little more to be said.

As I write this, so many long years after the events I have described, I too am now one of those elders who stands far from the bright flame of childhood, and near to the chill doors of eternity. Now it is I who must fill the role that Reverend Toivonen once filled, and counsel the rising generation that what seems to them long or even boundless will soon seem all too short.

Yet to say that life is short and fragile is not to say that it is worthless. Flowers bloom only briefly before they fade or are plucked, and yet their Creator saw fit to fashion them with great beauty. And it is a commandment often neglected (and needlessly so, for it is not a difficult one) that we are to live joyfully with those we love, all the days of our vanity, and all the days of our labor under the sun.

This I have endeavored to do.

I suppose that you will recall how, at the beginning of this narrative, I said that 2156 was the most important year of my life? Perhaps you are wondering why I did not say that it was 2163, the year my father and I pried that rusty barrel out of the sediments, and sent it to Ñork to be destroyed, and were lauded as heroes for saving Gwinn from ruin?

Yet none of that would have happened were it not for my earlier emergence from my youthful shyness, and for my having known so many pleasures of friendship back in 2156. It was because of 2156 that I felt like Enos Hartfeld was the last person in the world who would fritter away his virtue, rob his family, and abscond with a troupe of stage nomads—and it was because of 2156 that, when he did so anyway, I went looking for answers, and found them.

Thus the things that matter most to me are still my memories of Enos's bright voice as he called my name in the schoolyard or churchyard each morning, and his ingenuity when he convinced the other boys that the world's first electricity came from cats, and his quiet diligence as he worked long hours with Reverend Toivonen in the sacred vineyard, and his sense of wonder when he lost himself in the worlds within Adam Fau's books, and his excitement when he stripped off the last of his clothing and plunged, carefree and naked, into his favorite swimming hole.

These were the things that affected me the most. The memory of living joyfully in the days of our vanity was what moved me to action when action was required, and now, when action can do no more, it moves me to patience.

So it was when I mourned over what happened to Enos, and so it would be in my deeper times of sorrow, when I parted from my father and my mother, and when I and my wife laid three of our seven children to rest in the cold and silent earth.

And now, with most of my life behind me, I still await, patiently and fearlessly, the time when I will meet that grace which alone can heal the afflictions I have seen in my days.

Anna

I am, I think, one of the first people to know what it was that young Jacob Martin had found on that September day in 2163.

I did not, of course, know any sooner than the rest of Gwinn that Jacob had found a whole barrel full of poison, and that he and his relatives might well have saved us all by removing it from the little sheep pond before it could crack open. I learned that part of the story at the same time as everyone else, when the mayor announced it alongside that roving Afterling.

But when I saw Jacob wander onto my land from the direction of the place where the Hartfelds used to keep their sheep, and then collapse in the most perfect anguish beneath that ladder, and shed so many tears before sleep overtook him that he could have watered the grass all around him — when I saw all of that happening, I knew there must have been some logic to it.

And when I spoke with my brother Adam, the keeper of our family's books, we each found out the other half of the story. Jacob, it seems, had just learned what heavy metal poisoning was. And he had been close with Enos Hartfeld, years and years earlier, when Enos was a very different sort of boy than he would later become. Jacob had gone to find out whether the water up in the hills where Enos had been spending his summers was tainted, and the condition in which Jacob returned told me all that I needed to know.

For many years thereafter, I left Jacob's ladder in just the place where he had slept beneath it. And later, when the timbers of the barn it was leaning against rotted, and the barn had to be pulled down, I marked the place with a stone.

Jacob, by this time, had married and cleared a new farm for himself, a few miles to the south in Ironpin. But even when he was still in Gwinn, I do not think he ever returned to the place he had spent that one night after coming down from the northwestern hills.

But I always reverenced that place. It may not have been a battlefield worthy of bronze-tipped towers and marble monuments, like in the pictures I had seen in a few of my brother's books. Yet it seemed to me that the tears shed beneath that ladder had done at least as much to preserve my homeland as the blood shed on any field of battle.

Later on, when I was well into old age, I dreamed a dream by which I was persuaded that I and my husband should build an altar at that site. When the altar was finished, I told a few of my friends and kindred about it. I told them only that we had built it, not our reason for thinking the place sacred. Still, they knew my reputation for wisdom and piety, and they began to worship there.

It was not, of course, a place for blood sacrifices, for we Christians did away with those long ago. Yet there are still those among us who follow the old law of giving tithes of the fruits of the earth, and they came, from time to time, to pray at the altar and dedicate their harvest. And the people began to notice when flowers bloomed all around the altar, and when birds and woodland creatures drew near to it, and when the supplicants who prayed there were, in a great many cases, healed of their afflictions.

At present, no one but myself knows the tale behind this altar (my husband having already gone the way of all the earth), but I know that someone will find this leaf among my papers when I too am no more.

And whether this altar, after I am gone, becomes a pilgrimage site at the end of a beaten path, receiving the homage of all the hundreds who dwell in Gwinn, or whether its traffic dwindles until it is known only to us ghosts, and to the mute denizens of the forest, matters not to me.

One way or the other it will stand, as it has hitherto stood, as a testimony to an unfading lesson—to the same lesson that the Holy One taught us so many years ago—that when an innocent man suffers for the sins of the guilty, and a pure-hearted witness beholds it and comes away changed, it is through them that power is given to redeem the land.

Contributors

Bruna Nobrega (cover art) is an illustrator-artist from São Paulo, Brazil. She has degrees in both PR and digital marketing. Later she found her true vocation in art. Her work focuses on watercolor and mixed media. The muses are many, but Brazilian nature and medieval illuminated manuscripts are major inspirations.

Justin Patrick Moore's work has appeared in *Mythic: A Quarterly Science Fiction and Fantasy Magazine*, *Love in the Ruins: Tales of Romance in the Deindustrial Future*, and *Abraxas: International Journal of Esoteric Studies*. His essays on culture, subculture and a variety of other subjects appear frequently on his website sothismedias.com. He is also an avid radio hobbyist. Justin and his wife Audrey make their home in Cincinnati, the Queen of the West.

Pierre Magdelaine lives in France, where he writes stories of dichromat private eyes, paranoid structural engineers and adventurous shepherds, and dabbles at ceramics, such as the engraving printed atop his story (more on Instagram @pierremagdelaine). The turtle story in "The Mythmaker's Daughter" is a retelling of the cosmogonic myth of the Ojibwe people, and the old ballad Mary's husband used to sing is of course "Black is the Color (of My True Love's Hair)," a traditional Appalachian folk song. There might have been other sources of inspirations for the story: we are what we eat, and this particular writer's diet is full of all sorts of myths, tales and legends.

JJ Dettman was born, raised, and currently lives in the Greater Toronto Area. He happily spends much of his time trying to convince students that physics is fun, not scary. At other times, he can be seen at the local pub, coffee shop, or independent movie theater, or with books. Reading and writing fiction has always been a cherished pastime of his. The technology in this story was inspired by an actual project proposed for reducing the melt rate of a glaciers.

Eric Rust Backos lives in Lake County, Ohio where he practices Druidry and Green Wizardry. The setting—fictional Edwardtown, Ohio—and characters for this story sprang forth from a failed attempt to write an adventure module for John Greer's RPG Weird of Hali: Roleplaying the Other Side of the Cthulhu Mythos. The challenge accepted in the story is from *Green Wizardry*, also by Greer. Maple County turned out to be in a different universe than the RPG setting. Besides, some stories have their own ideas on how they want to be told...

Clint Spivey teaches English as a foreign language. While occasionally helping out on a rice farm he also tends a small garden of his own. His fiction has appeared in *New Maps* and is upcoming in the anthology *Haunted Trains: Creepy Tales from the Railways*. Fiction set in the future sometimes seems to him full of confident people basking in the thrill of the collapsed world. He wanted to explore the opposite of that, without trivializing the very real anxiety that comes from growing up in our current sick, predatory system. More lightheartedly, he was considering vision problems in the future, and the possibility that optometry might endure as a career.

C. M. Barnes lives and writes in New Mexico. His work has appeared in *American Short Fiction*, *Digital Americana*, *Booth*, and elsewhere. He is currently at work on a collection of speculative tales and is always fascinated by the way old stories are made new by a struggling, flailing, and hopeful world. Read more at silenceoncebroken.com.

Wesley Stine was born in Arizona to parents from Indiana. He currently lives in Georgia, where he is working toward a doctorate in physics at Emory University. Like many graduate students, he travels mainly by bicycle and he eats a lot of rice and beans. Wesley has been writing deindustrial fiction for a little more than a year, and "Jacob's Ladder" is his fourth story to see print. Outside of physics and writing, his favorite things to do include reading history, both ancient and modern, and composing classical music. His favorite historian is Herodotus, and his favorite composer is Beethoven.

Nathanael Bonnell grew up in turn-of-the-millennium Cincinnati and, after a long series of vagabonding adventures and misadventures, now lives with his partner Misty and baby son Ivor in Wisconsin's northwoods, where he wears hats from a steadily expanding collection, including "editor," "landscaper," "farmhand," and, most recently, "signpainter." His early years as a spelling bee kid (16th of 251 at nationals) served as a gateway drug to hardcore linguistics nerdery.

Comments for contributors sent to the editor will be forwarded.

COLOPHON

New Maps is typeset by the editor using an ancient, temperamental program called LaTeX which nevertheless produces unsurpassable results. The text font is an early digital version of Hermann Zapf's Palatino—resurrected from abandoned files and fitted with modern amenities like kerning tables and characters like Þ—which retains all the calligraphic warmth of the 1950s original cut that was lost in the production of the popular Linotype version. Titles are set in Sebastian Nagel's 2010 typeface Tierra Nueva, which is based on lettering from a 1562 map of the Americas; headers, drop caps, and miscellany are in Warren Chappell's classic Lydian. After various fonts trialed, the magazine has settled on Spline Sans Mono for URLs and the like.

ACKNOWLEDGMENTS

All of the thanks to Misty. Just all of them.